AN AVALON CAREER ROMANCE

FALCON'S RETURN
Rebecca K. O'Connor

With the whir of her camera's shutter blending with the sound of her heart beating, Brooke focused on her most enigmatic subject to date. Marshall Anthony stood as regal and proud as the beautiful peregrine on his arm and his amazing green eyes seemed to pierce her camera lens. She was certain she had found the perfect subject for award-winning photographs, but she was less certain about the man and his imperfections.

After an anxious search for his wayward falcon and a romantic sunset flight in his two-seater plane, Brooke found herself seeing the heart behind the rough exterior. There was something about the trust and compassion he held for his falcon that kept pulling her into his presence. Complicating matters, though, is her childhood buddy, Jeremy. Will she have to sacrifice her longest and closest friendship to find true love with Marshall? If she doesn't work something out soon, she may lose them both.

FALCON'S RETURN

•

Rebecca K. O'Connor

AVALON BOOKS
NEW YORK

PRINTED IN THE UNITED STATES OF AMERICA
ON ACID-FREE PAPER
BY HADDON CRAFTSMEN, BLOOMSBURG, PENNSYLVANIA

For Mom and Jaye, who taught me that I could
create something "right"
even when everything is going wrong.

Chapter One

It was a perfect picture, the sort that makes you forget to breathe until the shot is framed and the shutter clicks. The breeze ruffled the feathers on the back of the falcon's neck and her falconer's hair was tousled as well. The air seemed to adore them both. The falcon and her partner had an intense stare that spoke of something distant they both shared a longing for. Brooke thought they looked like kindred spirits as the shutter snapped and the film advanced. Then she choked on a breath as the falcon turned toward the noise and the man's eyes followed. The bird only gave her a quick glance, but the falconer's green eyes pinned her behind the lens and left her heart stuttering. She felt like she had been caught eavesdropping and lowered the camera slowly from her face. The eyes held her still and now her mouth was dry as well. Then he turned abruptly, slipped a hood on the falcon's head and they strode into the field.

He's arrogant, she thought. He's just plain full of himself. She turned to the woman standing next to her and asked, "Who is that?"

"That's Marshall Anthony." The woman glanced at her camera and nodded toward the field. "He's flying Shae and he won with her last year. You should get your camera ready."

"Thank you." The woman had turned away and it was obvious that she would answer no more questions. She was dressed in torn jeans and a t-shirt but looked lithe and stunning just the same. A tall redhead, she seemed the sort of woman who wouldn't give Brooke the time of day if she didn't have to. Brooke looked around and thought that it must be apparent that she didn't belong there. She had no idea they were going to be in the middle of a pasture. It seemed that something like a "Sky Trial" would be in some place grander, a stadium or at least in a high-school football field. She looked down at her favorite black leather boots and mourned the scuffs and dust. She had wanted to look professional. Perhaps she should have done her research instead. This was a place for ponytails and jeans; career casual was much too formal. It was, however, a photographer's dream of interesting faces and action. For the moment, the potential of it all escaped her. The only thing she could concentrate on was the image of two green eyes. She wished she had pressed the shutter when they had looked down her lens. That would be a photograph to keep, one for the bedside or under the pillow. She shook her head and forced herself to concentrate. She would never sell any photographs by drooling over arrogant men.

"This isn't just a hobby, Brooke. It's what you want to do with the rest of your life. Now pay attention." She chided herself under her breath, but the woman next to her gave her a sideways glance.

Jeremy had told her about the Sky Trials and urged her to go. He had thought it would be an incredible place for pictures and an even better story. He had her convinced that the story would sell. It was the history that made her want to go though. Falconry was from a time when chivalry still existed. Of course back then a woman wouldn't even be allowed to touch a falcon, but at least the gallant man with the bird on his glove would always come to rescue the damsel. That would be how she imagined it, anyway. Falconry was, after all, the sport of kings and princes. Princes with blazing green eyes.

"Stop it, Brooke." This time she was talking to herself clearly and the woman next to her was no longer pretending to ignore her.

"Are you all right?" The woman looked more concerned with herself than with Brooke's well-being.

"I'm fine. Thank you for asking." Brooke thought she was probably blushing and hid her discomfort by fiddling with her camera bag. It would be good to put the polarizer on the lens, if only to protect it from the dirt blowing around.

"He's putting her up now. You'll want to keep a close eye on her. It will be easy to lose sight of the falcon once she gets a good pitch."

Brooke was nodding, but the woman had already turned away. She knew the birds flew high. She could never hope to get a decent shot with the falcon in the air. In the field, Marshall Anthony had taken the hood off Shae's head once more and she clung to the glove, her wings paddling the air. Marshall's head was leaning slightly toward the falcon as if he were listening. They seemed to be warming up and strategizing. Brooke snapped another photo and imagined what it would be like to have a connection so easy with something so wild. How long would that take to learn? She took one more photo as Marshall nodded and Shae lifted off his glove. Her narrow wings moved her in a powerful spiral above her partner.

"Wow." Brooke let her camera fall, entranced by the strength in the bird's wings. "Look at her go."

"Pure anatum. She's a beautiful peregrine."

"What?" Brooke was surprised by the sudden warmth in the voice of the woman standing next to her.

"Anatum. It's a subspecies of peregrine. I think they are the most beautiful of all the peregrines in their adult colors and Shae is a beauty. That's for sure."

The woman spared Brooke a quick glance and a kind smile. Then she turned her eyes back to the field, the smile still on her face. Marshall was moving out into the field, waving his arm as if to urge the falcon to follow him. "Keep your eyes on her or you will lose her for certain. Have you ever seen a sky trial before?"

"No. I haven't." It was obvious this woman had seen many and Brooke found herself wanting to continue the conversation. "I'm a photographer. Well, I would like to call myself a professional photographer. I just need to start selling some photographs. I heard about this contest and thought there would be some incredible images here. I was right." The falcon was really starting to climb. Brooke wondered how in the world Marshall could still be connected with the bird. "If I were that high, I would never come down."

"She's getting up there." The woman paused to calculate. "She's maybe eight hundred feet." She pointed toward the bird. "It's called ringing up. Shae will probably sky out. I mean, she'll be so high you can't see her."

"How will he know that she is still there?"

"He doesn't have to know. He trusts her." Brooke looked at the woman in disbelief, but she was smiling like she was watching a sweet romance. "Wonderful to have a man trust you enough to let you sky out."

"You're right." Well, so much for first impressions. Brooke liked this woman and felt the same expression shape her own face. "My name is Brooke Sidelle."

"Mary Shannon. It's a pleasure to meet you." Mary reached for Brooke's hand without taking her eyes off the sky and laughed as they shook. "Can you still see her?"

"Yes, I think. Wow. She's really up there, isn't she?"

"That's what you want, Brooke. You want your bird to ring right up and wait on until you flush something for her to catch."

"From that height? How do you catch something?"

"You knock it out of the air." Mary was laughing again.

"Ouch." Brooke flinched and thought of the ground.

"It's what they're designed for." Mary's voice was reverent now. "A peregrine can dive over two hundred miles an hour. They definitely pack a punch."

"Wow. Talk about not knowing what hit you!" At least it would be over quickly. Brooke had never liked the idea of hunting, but you couldn't argue that the designs of nature were wrong.

"Marshall will be judged on how quickly his bird rings up, how high her pitch is, how quickly she responds and on the chase."

"The chase?" Just then another man in the field with Marshall threw something into the air.

"This chase." Mary grabbed her arm and pointed. "Don't worry, the pigeon has more than a fair chance."

"A pigeon!" Something white was moving away

from Marshall and the two other men in the field with him.

"There's Shae!" Mary's grip tightened and Brooke gasped. The falcon was tucked and falling from the sky in a blur. Just when Brooke was certain that the pigeon was going to get hit by the feathered meteor, the white bird darted to the side and out of harm's way. Collectively, the onlookers groaned. Brooke was holding her breath. Shae adjusted and the pigeon moved in the crowd's direction. It lost altitude and buzzed over their heads. Shae came screaming after it, the sound of her wings as loud as aircraft. She meant business, but the pigeon meant to survive.

"Nobody move!" One of the judges yelled at the crowd and they obediently held still. Brooke thought to herself that she couldn't move if she wanted to. The pigeon was weaving through the people, the peregrine hot on its tail. Then the white bird dove beneath a car and out the other side. The falcon got confused and landed, trying to see where its quarry had gotten off to. She must have seen it after a moment, because she followed once more, but it was too late. The pigeon had pulled away and was gaining distance.

"She doesn't have a chance in a tail chase like that. Her only real advantage was the fall." Mary sounded disappointed, but she laughed once more. "Now *that* was a pigeon that knows falcons. Marshall pulled himself a worthy opponent out of that cage. I guess you can't win every year."

"That was a good flight, though, right?" Brooke watched as Shae disappeared into the distance, still in pursuit. Marshall was waving and yelling in the bird's direction.

"Yes, but she needs to be back on the glove soon in order for Marshall to have any hope of winning this competition."

"Folks, it looks like it's telemetry time. Sit tight. We'll get on to the next bird as soon as Mr. Anthony retrieves his." The judge looked amused, but then this flight had been good sport.

"What does that mean, 'telemetry' time?" Mary turned away from Marshall who was waving his arms and obviously swearing, although they couldn't hear him. She gave Brooke her full attention.

"We fly our birds with transmitters. A falcon could be twenty-five miles away in a very short time. Marshall is getting out his receiver now."

"So he'll be able to find her then." Mary nodded. Marshall was pulling out a metal box from the back of a Suburban. He looked absolutely hot under the collar. Brooke thought she had rarely seen a man look that angry. Unable to resist, she raised her camera again and took another shot. Unbelievably, he turned in her direction and gave her a dirty look. "What, is he psychic or something?"

"What?" Mary gave her a confused look.

"Nothing." His anger began to make her uneasy. "Will he punish Shae when he finds her?"

Mary began to laugh. It really was a nice laugh and Brooke found herself hoping that they could be friends. "You could never punish a wild animal, Brooke, especially one that flies. Why, she would merely leave him. She'll come back to him and he'll forgive her. He's angry now, but he loves her." She had that romantic look to her eyes again and Brooke couldn't help but smile.

"What do you do for a living, Mary?"

"I'm a nurse." And she loved it, from the look on her face.

"ER?"

"No. No. Pediatrics. I'm a baby nurse." She made a cradle with her arms and nodded. "You said you want to be a photographer, but what are you doing to pay the bills in the meantime?"

"I'm a paralegal. I mean, I work for an attorney. I was on my way to law school, took the LSAT and everything, but it's not really what I want to do."

"Ah, it's what everyone else wanted you to do." Mary was tucking her hair behind her ears and it made her look innocent and sincere. Brooke thought that not only was she right, but she understood.

"Yes. Everyone but me. It's fine for now and I'm good at it, but I want to leave this world feeling like I've left something behind. A bunch of lawsuits isn't really what I have in mind."

Mary smiled and nodded, then nearly lost her balance as a golden retriever pushed against her leg and looked up at her with adoration. "Oh, Jake. When are you ever going to learn any manners?"

"Who's going to teach him? Certainly not you, and I don't have any to teach him." A handsome man with dark hair and blue eyes leaned over to kiss Mary, a falcon balanced on his left hand.

"Hello, Robbie." Mary looked embarrassed, but only for a second. "Rob, I want you to meet my new friend, Brooke."

"Nice to meet you." She shook his hand and watched his bird, worried it would feel the motion, but it didn't seem bothered. Then she looked at Mary, realizing she had just called her a friend and gave her a smile.

"Brooke, this is my husband Rob."

"You always do find the pretty girls, Mary. Who were you thinking of setting this one up with?" Rob winked at them both and turned his attention to the bird who was scratching at its hood.

"I wasn't thinking of setting her up with anyone, Robbie." She looked irritated, but her husband seemed amused. "She's a budding photographer and seems to really like the birds. I was thinking that you and I could take her out sometime. I'm sure she'll be done with this long-winger nonsense after today. I thought we could take her out to do some real flying with the Harris' hawks."

"Dirt hawking." Rob no longer looked amused.

"Call it what you will, but at least you can watch it without getting a kink in your neck."

"I would love to!" Brooke was a little worried that this was going to turn into a full-blown argument, but it was obviously an old discussion.

"We would love to have you out with us then. We'll call it a date." Rob nodded at Brooke and she couldn't help but smile back.

"Are you flying next?" The bird on Rob's fist was as white as the pigeon that had disappeared and looked relaxed.

"Yep. My girl is up next."

"She's a peregrine?" Brooke didn't think that per-egrines could be so pale.

"No, she's a gyr/peregrine cross. That's why she's so white and so big."

"That's why she's such a pain in the rump." Mary gave the bird a dirty look.

"No, that, my darling, is why she's named Mary."

"Hmmn." Mary crossed her arms against her chest and gave them both a glare.

"She's just jealous that she has competition." Rob raised his eyebrows at Brooke and gave her another mischievous wink. But it was obvious that Mary had no competition in the world.

"Would you both mind if I took your picture? I mean, all of you, the dog and the falcon too. It would be a great photograph."

Mary uncrossed her arms and moved closer to her

husband. "That's very flattering. Of course. You don't mind, do you Robbie?"

"No, of course not. It will be for posterity. Mary *is* going to win the sky trials, after all." The original Mary turned to give them both a dirty look and Brooke took one picture and then another as they all posed like they were completely blissful.

"Attention, Ladies and Gentlemen. We have just gotten a call that Mr. Anthony has his falcon secured. We will continue with the trials. Will the next falconer please join us in the field." The crowd hushed at the call of the judge and Rob gave Mary another kiss.

"Wish us luck, darling."

"You won't need luck, Robbie Shannon. That bird is a powerhouse. Just make sure you pick a good pigeon."

Rob walked toward the field and Mary leaned over to Brooke. "That bird will win. She flies with style. Robbie's only competition was Marshall. Cross your fingers."

"I will." Brooke imagined those blazing green eyes and wished the Marys luck anyway. "Did Rob introduce you to falconry?"

"Ha! I introduced him to falconry." She sounded offended and Brooke flinched.

"Oh, I didn't mean . . ." She wasn't sure what she didn't mean.

"No. It's okay. I'm just sensitive about that. Everyone always asked, 'Where's your boyfriend? Did someone teach you how to fly that bird?' If you ask me, a woman *knows* how to fly a bird. A man has to learn." Mary spoke like someone who had been flying birds for a lifetime and Brooke believed she knew what she was talking about, but she couldn't help but laugh. "You laugh, but it's true and I don't have to chase a falcon all over kingdom come to prove it."

"I would love to go out with you, Mary. It really does sound like fun." Brooke meant it too. The Shannons seemed like an extraordinary couple.

"There she goes." Mary pointed to the field where a white streak was circling Rob and moving into the sky. "It's late in the day for her, but it looks like she's going to do it. She's never let Rob down before." She was a much bigger bird than Shae, but it didn't seem to slow her down. "Robbie has only been flying long-wings for three years now. He's a real natural." Mary looked proud, but Brooke suspected she only looked this way when Rob couldn't see it.

"How long has Marshall been flying falcons? That's what you mean when you say 'long-wings,' right?"

"Yeah. Falcons are long-wings. Marshall?" She gave Brooke a quick look like she was sizing her up.

"What? I meant for the story, of course. I'm just looking for a good line." She was curious though, a little anyway.

"Marshall is a good line. I have to admit that. He's been flying falcons since he was a teenager. He comes from family money and I hear that's all he does. He just flies falcons."

"That's all he does? He's a professional falconer?"

"No. He gets paid for his lineage, not for his falconry. But, yes, that is what he does full time. At least, that's what I've heard." She sounded like she thought it distasteful, but Brooke couldn't help but wonder if it wasn't jealousy. She thought it was fascinating that a man would spend his entire existence focused on a sport that was thousands of years old.

"Speak of the devil." Mary jerked her head in the direction of Marshall who was walking up with his bird. "He shouldn't have that bird out while another is in the air. He might distract it." Mary spoke gruffly, but Brooke could tell she didn't really believe that Marshall could distract her husband's bird. "She's almost skied out!"

"Really?" Brooke looked for the white falcon in the glare of the sun but knew she didn't have any hope of finding it. She couldn't help it. She went back to watching Marshall. Mary had been right. He moved carefully with the bird on his glove. He never jarred her or even gave her a dirty look. He moved toward his Suburban without ever taking his eyes off of her. She was forgiven. She was more than forgiven. She was adored. Brooke wondered if he had been frightened. Maybe he thought he would never see her again. Maybe he had thought he lost her forever, but here she was on his glove and that was something to be grateful for. He tucked her into the back of the truck and briefly looked at the sky. Around her people were yelling, Mary was jumping up and down, and Brooke knew that Rob and his bird had just won.

Marshall turned his attention back to Shae and smiled as he pulled a piece of food out of the vest he wore and slipped off her hood. He hung the hood from his ear without a thought to being self-conscious and gave his bird her breakfast.

"They did it! I knew he could do it. Did you see that flight?" Mary was grabbing her arm and trying hard not to continue jumping.

"What? Oh no. I missed it."

"You missed it?" Mary stopped for a moment and turned to look at Marshall. "Oh, I see." She nodded at Brooke. Marshall looked in their direction and bowed his head graciously. "Thank you and well flown by you as well." Mary gave him a deep curtsey. Marshall couldn't have possibly heard her from the distance, but smiled like he had. "Let me introduce you to him."

"Oh, no. Mary, I don't really think that now would be the time." It was too late. Mary was already walking in his direction without even a glance back to see if she was being followed. "Wait, I don't think . . ." She was out of earshot as well. "Oh boy." Brooke began a brisk walk after her new friend. *It's just for a story.* He really would make a great story, but her heart was pounding and she wasn't convinced that was why she wanted to meet him.

Marshall Anthony was instantly standing very straight, his hands shoved in his pockets and his chin raised. Brooke considered turning around and heading in the other direction as Mary pointed and waved her over. It was obvious that the man wasn't pleased with the prospect of being accosted by two women. He didn't look as at ease without a bird on his hand. He moved with a stiffness that she hadn't noticed when he had held Shae. She had made up her mind to forget about the whole business of an introduction when Marshall gave her what she thought was a haughty look and turned his back to her. "So much for the charming falconer." She reached to take the lens cap off her camera, thinking she wouldn't mind playing the part of the irritating photographer.

"Marshall, I would like you to meet Brooke." Mary seemed oblivious to the man's sudden chill. "She's a photographer."

"Nice to meet you." He looked her in the eyes for merely a second and didn't offer his hand. Shae seemed to require his attention in the truck. There was a soft ringing, like sleigh bells coming from inside.

"What's that noise?"

"What noise?" He turned to look her in the face and his irritation faded for a moment. She hadn't noticed through the lens that he had such full lips and high cheekbones. His features were hard and smooth, as if he had been carved in stone and then smoothed over by the wind.

"That—that noise. The jingly sound. Like Santa or something." Oh that was clever. She was feeling like a regular Wordsworth.

"Oh, the bells." He turned away as if the conversation was over and he had explained everything to his satisfaction.

"What bells?"

"The falcon's bells, Brooke." Mary was studying them both and it made Brooke wonder what she was thinking. It obviously wasn't about bells, but she had decided to step in and save Marshall's side of the conversation anyway. "We put bells on the bird's legs a lot of the time so that we can hear where they are. We use one on each leg in different tones. It's a lovely sound, isn't it?"

"A hundred times better than Christmas." Marshall was clearly talking to himself or the bird because he certainly wasn't talking to either Brooke or Mary. It didn't make a difference because Brooke was talking to him whether he liked it or not.

"I don't know about that. All the sound of those bells means is sudden death to some unsuspecting flying creature." She didn't know why she had said it, but it was far too late to take it back. So she crossed her arms against her chest and prepared for the storm.

He was silent for several moments, unhooking the bells from the falcon's legs. "Maybe that's the most graceful way to die." Far from what she had suspected, his voice was soft and thoughtful. "And the greatest gift I've ever been given is the sound of these bells on a bird's return to the fist. It's the most delicate trust you could ever earn." He turned to the bird who was still eating with such dainty bites it was hard to believe she was a killer. "Of course, that's not something you could capture with something as sterile as a photograph."

"Really." Brooke wondered if he meant to be rude. He hadn't taken his eyes off the bird, so she couldn't really tell. "I guess photography does require a little imagination. I think I could capture that, you would just have to be willing to recognize art."

"And you're thinking I'm too uncultured to appreciate art?" He turned to look her in the face, eyebrows arched, challenging her to confirm his statement.

"Marshall?" Mary was no longer examining the both of them. She looked ready to diffuse an argument.

"Well, Mary told me that you would have plenty of time to take me out to see your bird fly again if I asked you. There's too much activity here to get a decent shot. You're more than welcome to see my photographs when they're developed. I'm quite good and we could revisit this discussion then." I'm quite good? She wasn't certain she was any good at all, but she squared off her shoulders and raised her chin at him.

"Plenty of time?" He turned his face toward Mary and narrowed his eyes. "Why would that be?"

"I told her that you always had time for a pretty girl." Mary didn't even looked ruffled. Brooke breathed in with relief that she had backed up her story.

"I don't have time for 'girls' at all, but I certainly wouldn't back down from something that sounded like a challenge."

"Then you're on." Brooke didn't like the way he said "girls." It sounded like an insult, but she wasn't one to back down either.

"Mary, I'm sure you have my number somewhere. You can give it to, what did you say your name was?"

"Brooke. Brooke Sidelle." She grabbed his hand and shook it before he had a chance to withdraw. He paused for a moment and looked into her face. He held her there like he was looking for something. She found herself wishing she knew what it was.

"You'll want to wear something a little more appropriate when you come out hunting with me, Brooke."

"Well." She didn't like the way he said "Brooke" either, come to think of it. "Life isn't a rehearsal, you know. It doesn't hurt to dress for it. I don't suppose that matters to you, though."

"Life is something more than a play, Miss Sidelle. Let me know when you have a free moment on your calendar and can find an old pair of jeans." He was looking at her boots and smirking.

"You'll be hearing from me soon, Marshall Anthony, don't you worry." Brooke turned without another look and strode away with her head high, ignoring Marshall's soft laughter.

Chapter Two

"Wow." Marshall scratched his head and watched the blond kicking up a trail of dust behind her scuffed leather boots. "She's excitable."

"I'm sure she would say the same about you." Mary looked Marshall up and down, choosing to hold her tongue.

"Pretty girl. Can't say I think much of her personality though." Actually he admired the feisty blond's backbone. Pretty was hardly the word for her either. She was stunning. She was overdressed for the Sky Trials but she certainly knew how to dress herself. Her clothes were understated, but flattering. She had managed to tone down her curves. Still, they were unmistakably there.

"You certainly seem to bring out the best in her,

20

Marshall." Mary had one hand on her hip and the other was tucking her hair behind her ear. "I suppose I should go catch her if I'm going to give her your number. Are you in the club directory?"

"What?" He had forgotten Mary was there for a moment. Picturing Brooke in torn jeans and a baseball cap, he was lost in a smile. "Yes. It's in the directory. By all means go catch her. I can't wait to see the artwork of a master photographer."

"Did you tug on ponytails when you liked girls in grade school?" Now Mary had both hands on her hips, but her eyes were shining with mischief.

"What do you mean?"

"Never mind." Mary shook her head. "I know you long-wingers like to keep to yourself, but maybe you should come have dinner with Robbie and me some night."

"Yeah, maybe." He was still watching Brooke's departure and Mary thought it would be pointless to try to continue any intelligent conversation.

"I'll call you sometime." He merely nodded but Mary didn't look to see the acknowledgement. She took off after Brooke.

Brooke's irritation was obvious when Mary caught up to her at her car. Rearranging cameras and lenses in her bag, she was more than a little rough with her equipment. Mary cleared her throat and Brooke stopped shoving things into her bag. Realizing what she was doing, she shook her head.

"It's apparent that man is from money. He certainly doesn't know how to behave around us common folk." Brooke had a flush to her cheeks that hadn't been there before.

"No, I think it would be safe to say that Marshall prefers the 'common folk'. He's a falconer. They can be a little rough around the edges."

"Rough? He's downright abrasive. Falconers must be the rudest people I've ever met!" Realizing what she had just said Brooke's flush took over her face. "Except for you and Rob, of course." Really, Marshall hadn't been that terrible, he had just gotten to her somehow.

"Are you kidding? Robbie can be just about the rudest person I know." Mary was laughing softly. It was obvious that she hadn't been offended, but Brooke felt terrible anyway.

"I'm sorry. I didn't mean that. I'm just upset. I'm sure that most falconers are wonderful. I don't usually let people get to me so easily. I don't know why I'm so irritated."

"Don't get mad, get even. I can't wait to see the photos you take."

"Oh, I don't know, Mary." Brooke felt a small dread settle in. Perhaps she had bitten off more than she could chew. "I shouldn't have said that. Birds are tough to catch on film. I don't know how well I would fare. I haven't been taking photos all that long. People tell me that I have an eye for composition, but I'm still learning."

"I could be wrong, but I suspect that you're a natural. You just have to spend a little bit of time learning to read behavior and then you will be able to catch some brilliant shots. Have a little faith."

"It's not the faith I'm worried about, it's the ability." Brooke kept her eyes down, not wanting to take them off of her camera bag.

"Only someone who really wants something badly would be that afraid to fail. And it's that fear that would make you a fool for not trying." Mary said this softly, but with a great deal of conviction. Brooke felt something in her chest tighten up. "Robbie is a high-school teacher and I heard him say that to a student once. Be brave, Brooke. You have nothing to lose. And think of the satisfaction you'll find in showing Marshall Anthony the best of your work."

"I could lose a little bit of pride, I guess."

"So you made it into a challenge. There's some value to that if it will get you to the next step. And if it doesn't pan out the way you were hoping, it's only Marshall."

"Yeah, only Marshall." That was perhaps her biggest worry of all. She had been very careful about who she showed her art to, seeking out people she felt would only be supportive while being honest. She couldn't afford to have her burgeoning creativity squashed by a cruel word from the right person. Jeremy had been begging to see her portfolio, but Brooke had only been willing to show him the two photographs that had placed in local competitions. How wise would it be to share her creative efforts with an abrasive, rude, close-minded falconer? Even if he did have the most amazing eyes she had ever seen. She shook her head to clear the image from her mind.

"I got to thinking and I believe that the number in the directory is my old one. You would be better off reaching me on my cell phone anyway. I'm rarely near the phone at home." Brooke and Mary both whirled around and must have shared the same defensive look because Marshall took a step back, pulling the little piece of white paper against his chest. "You were still planning on calling me, right?" He reached out with the paper and waved it like a white flag. Brooke nodded and took the piece of paper cautiously.

"I assume you hunt on the weekends?"

"I do, but we start early. It might interfere with your beauty sleep." He gave her a mischievous smile. Brooke sighed. So much for the white flag theory.

"You don't normally get any beauty sleep then?" Brooke returned his smirk and raised an eyebrow.

"It's not something I concern myself with." Nor should he, Brooke thought. Marshall looked as if he thought the same.

"It's a shame. A little sleep might help with your disposition." Brooke shoved the number into her pocket and glanced at Mary. Mary's eyes were wide and she had her hands over her mouth covering what Brooke suspected might be a smile.

Marshall threw his head back and laughed. "How does Saturday strike you then? We would be meeting at dawn. Call me on Friday night and I'll give you directions to the field we fly in."

"Done."

"Good. I'll expect you to call. And when we go hunting, I expect you to be on time."

Brooke shook her head, preparing a retort, but he had rushed off before she could say another word.

"I guess that settles it, Brooke. You'll have to give it a go." Mary looked absolutely delighted.

"Me and my big mouth."

"Well, it's hard not to respond to a hard tug on your ponytail."

"What?" Brooke looked confused.

"Boys seem to think that if you like a girl, the best way to get her attention is to tug on her ponytail." Mary smiled as she noticed her husband's approach.

"Are you preaching about the evil ways of men again, Mary? I keep telling you that's the way you women like us." The falcon on his glove was enjoying her victory feast.

"This is true, Robbie." Mary gave him a kiss on the cheek and an affectionate glance to the bird. "Congratulations. I don't think there's any doubt as to who won the Sky Trials."

"We'll find out tonight at the banquet." It was obvious he was trying to be humble, but he was absolutely beaming. "Marshall come over to give his congratulations as well? Or did you set him and Brooke up on a date?"

"I didn't." Mary tried to cover the fresh redness to her face by giving her attention to the golden retriever who was just joining the party. Mary diligently scratched him behind the ears. "They worked things out on their own."

"Things?" Rob gave Brooke an inquisitive look.

"Well, it's not a date. I wouldn't even consider a date with that man." She kicked at the dirt with her shoe and thought she heard Mary stifle a giggle. "He might make for some good photography and maybe a story so I'm going to go out hunting with him."

"I see." He looked at Mary like he knew there was a lot more to the tale. They seemed to have a silent exchange that ended with, "I'll tell you about it later."

"I would still very much like to go out with the both of you as well."

"Of course. Actually, we would love to have you over for dinner some night. Robbie, do you think that next week would be okay?"

"Sure, no problem."

"What about next Thursday? Would that be good for you, Brooke?"

"That would be really wonderful, thank you."

"Well, then I'll expect to see you next week." Mary

reached out and gave Brooke a hug. "It really was a pleasure to meet you, my dear. I hope you and I will see each other fairly often." She scribbled down a number and Brooke slipped it into the same pocket she had shoved Marshall's into.

"Thank you for explaining things to me, Mary. I can't tell you how helpful that was." Brooke was sincere and she hoped that it showed.

"I suspect there is much more to explain to you." Mary giggled and gave Brooke's arm a quick squeeze. Then she grabbed Rob's hand and walked away with a wave, Jake keeping a respectful distance behind them. Brooke watched them go. She felt a little wistful as Mary leaned her head into Rob's shoulder, her auburn hair spilling across his back. From the distance their laughter reached Brooke, ringing in two different tones, just like a falcon's bells. Brooke began a silent list of all the things that were missing in her life and it started with the gentle promise of bells.

The second day of her weekend had been spent with the TV remote in one hand and something to eat in the other. She couldn't concentrate well enough to do much more than surf and chew. She had burnt the last two shots on her roll of film on meaningless subjects. Then she had rushed the slides in to be developed, thinking she had never been so impatient to get a roll of film processed before. All day Sunday as she flipped through the channels, her mind moved from one image she had viewed through the lens to the next. She never saw what was on the television at all. She had hoped the pace of a Monday at work would get her mind to cease its endless wandering and focus for a bit. She was having no such luck.

"Brooke, Jeremy is on the phone." The copy machine stopped the soothing whir of pushing paper and began slamming staples into the copies.

"Carol, just tell him that I'll call him back." Brooke scratched her head with the pen in her hand and sighed.

"I would be happy to tell him that you'll never be calling him again if you would like, but if you think you'll be talking to him, you should just take the call. He'll only be calling back in a half an hour anyway." There was pure acid in the woman's voice, but Brooke was used to it. "By the way, you left this in your printer." Carol handed Brooke the sheet of paper and smoothed her pink sweater over her stomach. "Is this part of the complaint you just collated?"

"Oh no." She really was having trouble concentrating. "I'll fix it."

"Of course you will, but first you can get rid of that man on the phone." Carol sounded disgusted and Brooke laughed. It was the same tone that Marshall had used to say "girl."

"He's not so awful, Carol. He's a pest I admit, but he's not that bad."

"I disagree. I just don't understand how you could

continue to talk to a man that stood you up at the altar. He's a worm."

"He didn't stand me up at the altar. You're being melodramatic."

"He may as well have. You were a wreck for months." Carol had her arms crossed over her chest and Brooke could see there was no arguing with her.

"I wasn't a wreck. He just cancelled the wedding. He apologized and we're friends now." Knowing how ridiculous that sounded, she could only mumble it and push past the older woman to escape into her office. Brooke had wanted to cancel the wedding herself, Jeremy had just beaten her to it and that was a long time ago. She sat down at her desk and took a moment to rub her temples. Jeremy had been calling her all weekend, according to the caller ID. For the first time in a very long time, if not ever, she had been avoiding him.

"Thank you for holding, this is Brooke."

"Brooke, where in the world have you been? I've been calling you all weekend."

"I've just been busy, Jeremy. What's up?"

"What's up? That doesn't sound like you. What's with the attitude?"

"I'm just tired." Attitude? Brooke rubbed her temples a little harder and told herself she *was* just tired.

"You sound tired. Are you sure there's nothing wrong?"

"No, nothing is wrong." Actually, she wasn't so sure that nothing was wrong. It seemed to her that something was missing in her life. She suspected that this something came with green eyes and an attitude of his own.

"How was your weekend?"

"It was good, Jeremy. Thank you for the tip about the Sky Trials. I think I might have gotten some great shots."

"I would love to see them when you have them."

"Well, if they're any good I'll show them to you." Cradling her forehead in the palm of her hand, she let her face fall close to her desk and waited for his sulking to begin.

"You never show me any of your pictures, Brooke."

"They are photos, Jeremy, not pictures. I've shown you the ones that have turned out well."

"Two pictures." She could almost see his lips pushed into a pout and his eyelashes blinking low like they were too heavy to lift. That look had worked on her in the past and she couldn't help but smile.

"Not all the shots turn out, Jerm. It's part of the business."

"You would think that at least a few of them would."

"If they do, I will show them to you. Look, I really need to get going. I'm behind."

"Wait. Brooke, I need to talk to you. Can we have lunch or something?"

"I can't today, but tomorrow I could."

"Brooke, I need to talk to someone now. Camille

called on Saturday. She wants to get back together. I don't know what to do. I'm supposed to call her tonight."

"Oh Jerm." The last thing she wanted to do today was spend her lunch discussing the virtues of the airheaded Camille. Still, he was her friend and if he really needed her she should be there for him. She sometimes wondered if she wasn't just a little jealous of simple Camille, with her porcelain skin and perfect black hair. That girl had probably never had a split-end in her life. "I don't know."

"You're my best friend, Brooke. I need to talk to someone. I would do the same for you." Right now he would be all eyes and they would be wide with desperation.

"I know you would. All right, but it has to be close and it's not going to be a long lunch."

"Okay. I'll meet you at Delia's at noon."

"Fine, Jeremy. I'll see you later." She hung up the phone and sighed. They had been confidants since Jerm had dropped dirt down her back in third grade. She had been there for him when his mother died in junior high. He had been there for her when her parents got divorced in high school. He was the sort of friend that was difficult to come by. In a lifetime, you could count those sorts of friendships on one hand. It would be stupid to let something as simple as a broken engagement ruin their relationship. She shook her head at herself and got up to get a cup of coffee. A woman who thought at twenty-six that a broken engagement was something simple was probably well on her way to becoming a spinster.

"Well, did you tell him where to go?" A splash of coffee hit the counter as Brooke poured herself a cup. She winced, unsure if she was wincing over the loss of coffee or Carol's grating voice.

"Yes, Carol. I told him he could go to lunch with me."

"You told him—oh, Brooke. You're such a pretty girl. Why do you waste yourself with that boy?"

"We've been friends for a long time. I would hardly call it a waste." She was right when she called him a boy though. He had always been a boy and Brooke had always taken care of him.

"You can't expect to find another man when you spend the majority of your time with your ex-fiancé."

"I know, Carol. I think that maybe we have discussed this before." There were times when Brooke regretted confiding in the woman and this was definitely one of them. When you spend all day every workday with someone, it's hard not to let them in on your life. Still, she often wished that she had a little bit more willpower and could just keep her mouth shut around the busybody blond.

"Yes, but you don't listen. You are such a pretty girl. If you would act like you were single, I am sure that the right man would come along."

"Maybe there's no 'right man,' Carol. Or maybe

there is, but our paths might never cross. I'm not going to forsake an old friendship because I'm holding on to a fantasy."

"That's a shame. The fantasy is worth it." Carol turned her attention to her coffee cup and dismissed Brooke with a wave of her hand. She muttered "Definitely worth it" as she returned to her office.

Brooke had been working with Carol for five years now. They were the only two legal assistants to Don Bartell, Attorney at Law, and his young practice. The business had changed a lot in the last few years and Brooke suspected that she had as well. Carol, however, had not. The woman had an ageless face and a mothering demeanor, but no children. It was a shame. She had plenty of practice with other people's children and would have been exactly what Brooke feared in a mother-in-law. Well, there was always something to be thankful for, wasn't there? At least Carol wasn't her mother-in-law.

Brooke nibbled at a turkey and Swiss cheese sandwich, thinking that she had lost her appetite. It sounded like Camille was back in grand style. Jeremy sounded so forlorn, that she couldn't help but feel sorry for him. Still, she had been enjoying doing things as a twosome instead of being the third wheel in outings. It was nice not having a problem deciding on what movie to see or which restaurant to go to. Unbelievably, Camille was more wishy-washy than

Jeremy had ever been. Or maybe it was that she would rather have Jeremy to herself.

"She says that she just can't do it alone anymore."

"Do what alone, Jerm?"

"Life. Just being. She asked me for some time and I gave it to her, but she's done with that. Her grandmother just died last month and I guess she's reevaluated her life a little. I think that if she needs me, maybe I should be there for her."

"Are you sure she really wants to be with *you*, or is it that she just can't stand to be alone?" Brooke tried to ignore the hurt look on Jeremy's face. "She said that she can't do it alone anymore, she didn't say that she couldn't do it without you."

"She wants to be with me, Brooke, otherwise she would get someone else."

"I'm not trying to be mean, Jerm. I just don't want you to get hurt again."

"Whenever I've asked you to be there for me, you have always been there. I think that I should do the same for her."

"Are you saying that I taught you that?"

"Yes, you taught me to be a good friend."

"Jeremy, with Camille it's different."

"How?" He was getting the flush to his face that promised he was about to get very angry.

"She hasn't been good to you. She should deserve to have someone like you and she doesn't."

"So who does deserve me?" The color was leaving his face. "Are you jealous?"

"No!" She wrapped her sandwich up. Now she really had lost her appetite. "Look, if you feel that you need to, maybe you should give your relationship another shot, but please be careful."

"Sometimes I think that you're the only person that really looks after me, Brooke. Thank you. I don't know what I would do without you." He stretched across the table and grabbed her hand. She looked into his eyes and could feel him reaching. It made her a little uncomfortable. "You really are the best." He had the sweetest smile. It was easy to see how anyone could be taken with it. Still, she often thought he had a lot of growing up to do. "Tell me about your weekend. Were those birds something else or what?"

"Yeah, the birds were really incredible." She looked down at the table and tugged the white paper wrapper a little tighter around the sandwich.

"You met somebody."

"No." She lifted her head and looked him directly in the face. She was trying to look indignant, but he didn't seem to be buying it. "Well, I met a few people. They were very nice."

"They seem like a rough bunch, falconers."

"Some of them definitely were." She smiled despite herself. "At least around the edges. I met a wonderful couple though. They are going to take me out hunting with them with some sort of hawk. It's different than hunting with falcons, I guess."

"That will be interesting. You got all the pictures you wanted of falcons, then?"

"Well, no, not really." She was playing with her sandwich wrapper again. "I'm going back out to get some more falcon shots."

"This couple has a falcon then as well?"

"Yes, but I'm not going with them." It was obvious where he was leading her but she really didn't want to get into this with him. Now, she thought *he* looked jealous.

"Who's taking you out with a falcon then?" His eyes narrowed and he tilted his head.

"Marshall Anthony. He's been flying falcons most of his life. I thought he might make a good story." She lifted her chin up and looked him in the face.

"Is he one of the 'rough' falconers you said you met?"

"Yes, as a matter of fact he is absolutely insufferable. He makes a great photo subject though." He makes a great subject! What was she thinking?

"I thought you didn't have your pictures back yet. How do you know what a good subject he is?"

"I just know." Well, he did take a great photo, no doubt, even scowling at the camera.

"I see." Jeremy was nodding his head. Brooke could see that the wheels were turning. "Does he think that you're insufferable too?"

"I suppose." She giggled and covered her mouth with her hand. "I did tell him he needed help with his disposition."

"His what?"

"I told him he has an attitude problem." She couldn't stop laughing.

"Really. You sound kind of comfortable with him considering you just met." He was obviously sulking.

"Comfortable?" Brooke stopped laughing. "Now *you're* jealous!"

"No." Jeremy moved his chair back a little, looking surprised. "I'm not. I'm just looking out for you. I mean, you know. Your dad isn't around and you don't have any brothers. Maybe I should chaperone you."

"What! Don't be ridiculous, Jeremy. I don't need a chaperone." She gestured at his slight build. "I would probably just end up defending both of us."

"Now, that's insulting." He pulled his arms across his chest and slipped into a pout. "And I'm not jealous."

"Well, neither am I." She sighed and smiled at him. "Just be careful."

"You too." They sat for a few moments in silence, neither sure where the conversation should go, finally deciding to talk about getting the check.

When they left, Brooke got into her car feeling more confused than she had in a long time around Jeremy. They had been through so much together. She had a vivid memory of his head in her lap, choking on tears that she couldn't stroke away. She had barely made his words out through the sobs, but she had answered with a promise that she would never leave him like his mother did. His mother hadn't meant to die, but it had hurt her heart just the same. It was a promise that she wouldn't break. It had meant too much to her. She hoped she would never have to choose between her best friend and someone else that she loved. Brooke wasn't sure that was a choice she could make.

Chapter Three

On Wednesday night Brooke sat at her kitchen table with the cordless phone in her hand and two neatly printed phone numbers in front of her. Both were on torn pieces of white paper and both had come out of the front right pocket of the pants she had worn to the Sky Trials. She had no idea which number was the Shannons, and which was Marshall's.

She had tried looking in the phone book, but there were no Shannons listed at all. Of course Marshall wasn't listed either. She thought that it should be obvious by the writing which one had been written by Mary, but the numbers on both strips of paper were nearly identical. Brooke wondered if all falconers wrote their numbers the same. Maybe you could tell a born falconer with handwriting analysis. She copied the printing from one of the strips of paper on a scratch pad and decided that she would be a better photographer.

Chewing on the end of the pen, she knew she was procrastinating. She really wanted to confirm dinner with the Shannons for the next night and get directions. If she chose the wrong number, she would probably end up talking to Marshall. She should have given them her number instead. Well, there was only one thing to do. She turned the two strips of paper upside down and mixed them around on the tabletop. Then she picked one, turned it over and dialed it into the phone.

The number immediately began to ring, so she figured it probably wasn't a cell number. That was a relief. Or was it?

"Yeah." The greeting on the other end of the line made it obvious that she hadn't gotten the Shannons' home.

"Hi, um, Marshall?"

"Yeah."

"This is Brooke."

"Brooke." He wasn't going to make this easy, was he?

"I'm sorry, I didn't mean to call you. I wasn't sure which number was yours and which was Mary's. I—"

"Okay then. I'll talk to you some other time."

"Wait!" She couldn't believe he would brush her

off like that. She figured he would want to talk to her for at least a moment. Apparently she had been wrong. "I thought since I had you on the line, we may as well confirm for this weekend."

"I can't confirm that right now. Call me when it gets closer."

"What? Why can't you confirm now?" She took a deep breath, surprised that she had questioned him like that. Normally she would have just rolled over and said she would call some other time if she had gotten the brush-off like that. What had gotten into her?

"I just may not be able to go."

"Did you forget you had another date planned or something?"

"Another date? Who said we had a date? Look. I just offered to take you because you wanted to get some shots of the bird." He sounded agitated and she felt her face warming with embarrassment.

"I didn't mean to imply that we had a date." She must have sounded hurt, because he softened his voice.

"Look. Date or no date, if I don't have a bird, we won't be out hunting."

"Oh. I'm sorry." Maybe he wasn't being rude for the sake of being rude after all. "What happened to Shae?" She was nearly whispering, a little afraid of the response.

"I just haven't seen her in a while." Did the man always have to be so vague?

"How did you lose her and where did she go?" If she wanted answers, apparently she was going to have to ask all the questions.

"I lost her signal yesterday. She was being chased by a wild Prairie falcon."

"Would it hurt her, the other falcon I mean?"

"I doubt it. She just wanted Shae out of her territory. For some reason Shae just decided to keep going."

"And you have no idea where she is?"

"No." The hard edge was gone. He sounded miserable.

"What will you do?"

"I'll find her." He didn't seem convinced.

"Is there anything that I can do to help?" She hoped she didn't sound stupid. There was probably nothing that she could do, but she meant it. She wanted to help.

"Well." There was a long pause. Brooke thought that maybe he was just being polite. Trying to think of a nice way to say, what could you possibly do to help me? "How do you feel about flying?"

"Flying?" Brooke pictured Shae's dive from invisibility and shuddered.

"Have you ever been in a Cessna?"

"Is that one of those little planes?"

"Yes. Mine only seats two people. Would that make you nervous?"

"No, of course not." Well, it would make her a little nervous, but he wouldn't be the man to admit it to.

The thought of him piloting the plane made her feel a little more at ease though. "You have a plane?"

"Yeah. I should have taken it up yesterday. I was just so sure that I would find her. I could use someone to help me with the telemetry."

"I would love to help you, but I don't know how I would be with something so technical." It did sound very technical. She knew she didn't have a mechanical mind and had no desire to give Marshall one more thing to give her a hard time about.

"Do you have an RPM meter on your car?"

"Yes." She shook her head, trying to understand where this was going. Hopefully he didn't want her to fly the plane instead.

"Can you read it?"

"Of course I can read it," she growled at him, sure that he was back to insulting her again.

"It's a done deal then. You can read a receiver."

"It's that simple?"

"Well, it's a little more complicated than that, but not much. You seem like a smart girl. I'm certain you could figure it out. I could use your help."

"Okay." That had done it. The first compliment she had been given, even if he had called her a girl. "Where do I meet you?"

"Can you make it to Flabob in a half an hour?"

"Flabob?!"

"Yeah, is that a problem? Because I could make a

few calls and find someone else to help me." There he was again with the attitude.

"It's just, well, that man crashed into Mount Roubidoux flying out of there last year."

"Yes, but he did it intentionally."

"He did?!"

"He did. We can discuss it in the plane if you would like. It's a pretty easy mountain to miss. It's more like a hill after all. Can you make it or not?" He didn't seem to have much patience.

"Yes, it will take me about forty minutes though. Will you wait for me?" This was a reasonable question. She wasn't too sure that he would wait.

"I'll wait, but only for about forty-five minutes. I've wasted too much time all ready."

"I'm leaving now." Wow, a five-minute cushion. Maybe he did like her a little bit.

"See you there." He didn't pause for a response. She only heard the phone click off.

"Oh, no." She sucked in her breath and squeezed her eyes shut. She hadn't called Mary and Rob yet.

She turned over the other slip of paper and dialed it in a hurry, scribbling Mary's name on it. She wasn't going to play guessing games with the numbers again.

"Hello?"

"Mary?"

"Yes, this is Mary."

"Hi, Mary. This is Brooke. I'm just calling to see if we were still having dinner tomorrow."

"Brooke! I'm so glad you called. I was hoping you would. Of course dinner is still on. Do you want directions?"

"Yes, but I'm in a hurry. Would it be all right if I called you tomorrow before I leave to get them? I really have to run."

"Certainly, is everything okay?"

"Yes." Brooke took a deep breath. She probably did sound a bit harried. "I'm on my way out to the airport to meet with Marshall. He lost Shae. I'm going to help him. With the telemetry."

"Oh no! I hope you can find her. How long has she been out?"

"Just since yesterday."

"I hope he had fresh batteries in the transmitters. He should still have a decent signal off of them if they were new. Good luck."

"Thanks." There was a pause while Brooke was thinking she didn't know that the transmitters used batteries, but they would have to, wouldn't they?

"With Marshall, huh? I'll be interested in hearing all about that tomorrow." Brooke could hear her smile.

"Certainly. I'll call you when I get home from work." They hung up the phone and Brooke grabbed her jacket off of the back of a chair and ran for her car.

Brooke had no doubt that the plane would be on its way down the runway at exactly forty-five minutes after they had hung up the phone. She wound down through the Chino Hills road with the turns as fast and tight as the Jetta could handle. It was a good pace. She just hoped she didn't have to talk her way out of any tickets.

She was worried about the falcon. She hadn't realized how truly spectacular a creature she was until she had gotten back her slides. A few of her shots had turned out gorgeous. She could see Shae's eager look to the sky, her body ready to spring from the falconer's glove. The ageless eyes and regal pose seemed enough proof that the bird could manage on her own. Still, it would be heartbreaking to have to worry about any danger threatening such an incredible bird. It only seemed right to be there to help Marshall if she could. No matter how difficult he could be. She knew she wanted to find that falcon. She also knew she wanted to find what it was the falcon trusted in the man.

There was one slide where you could see that relationship between the two, their eyes both focusing on the same object in the distance. You were almost certain that they could read each other's thoughts. The rich cap that colored the falcon's head matched the shade of Marshall's hair. Both of them were shaped by lines and shadows that hinted at a royal pedigree. Brooke was certain it was the best photo she had ever taken. It told a story about two creatures capable of being both brutal and graceful; who managed to forge a relationship on what was beautiful in them both. Looking at that slide gave her chills. It was a picture she would be willing to share with Jeremy. She wondered if Jeremy had managed to sort things out with Camille. There hadn't been any news from him and she reminded herself that she wasn't really jealous. She told herself it was only that her best friend had found someone and she hadn't yet. Then she thought of Marshall again and wondered if she had.

She made it to the airport in thirty minutes and found Marshall in ten. He was standing by the Cessna keeping a close eye on his watch.

"I didn't think you would make it."

"Well, I did." She had harbored a few romantic thoughts about Marshall gushing "thank you" when she arrived, but those were swept away in an instant.

"Get in the plane. We don't have a lot of light left. It would be good to figure out exactly where she is in the daylight."

Brooke nodded and climbed into the plane. They taxied down the runway and Marshall got the aircraft into the air with ease. "Do you like flying?" she shouted over the engine noise.

"Not really."

"Why not?" This surprised her. She imagined that he would want to fly more than anything.

"I got my license so that I could chase falcons. There is nothing beautiful about a big piece of metal mounting the sky. It's a human aberration. We don't really fly. We force the elements."

"Oh." She was stunned by his moments of poetry. It was a surprising contrast to his gruffness.

"There's a receiver at your feet. It looks a little bit like a gun. Let me level off and I'll show you how to use it."

"This here?" It did look a little like a gun.

"The antenna is folded up, but we don't need it. It's hooked to an antenna on the roof right now. We're just looking for a general direction to head in."

"I see." Brooke pointed it toward the floor and looked at the knobs on the back. She found a button on the handle and pushed it. The receiver made a sound like static.

"Okay. Good, you turned it on. Now watch this meter. The receiver will beep but it may be hard to hear in the plane. The higher the needle bounces the stronger the signal. As soon as you get anything let me know. I've already got it tuned in to her frequency."

"Understood." She looked down to see the town crystal clear below them. She had never been in a small plane before. It was amazing. Very loud, but she felt free. It may not be flying like a bird, but it must be a close second. She took one last good look and turned her attention to the meter on the receiver. She suspected that she might be staring at it for a while.

"Have you ever been married?"

"What?!" She took her eyes off the meter for a second to see if he was serious. He was looking forward, but he seemed to be waiting for an answer. "Have I ever been married?" He nodded his head. "No. What about you?"

"No. I've been told I'm for the birds." It sounded like a joke, but his tone told her it wasn't. She couldn't tell if that was the way he wanted it. "How old are you, twenty-five?"

"Twenty-six. What about you?" She was surprised that he had tried to guess her age, but didn't want to try herself.

"I'll be thirty in a few months." Wow. That made her think that thirty was sneaking up on her as well.

"That's a good age." It would be a good age, she thought. She was working up the courage to ask if he had a girlfriend when she saw the meter move. She didn't quite trust her eyes, so she waited before she said anything about it. There it was again. "We've got a faint signal."

"Good. Let me know when it gets a little stronger and we'll start trying to get a direction on it."

"Okay, I'll let you know." She waited for the needle to move again and there was nothing. Marshall was silent and seemed unperturbed as the minutes passed.

"You're sure you saw a signal, right?"

"I'm positive." She was doubting herself now, but didn't want to admit it.

"Okay. We're going to head a little more west and see if we can get it that way."

"Right. I'm watching." There was still nothing and

Brooke felt restless. The falcon was out there somewhere, but she was starting to think it wouldn't be so
easy to find her as Marshall implied. "What if she's
moving?"

"Well, at this time of the day with the sun going
down, the hope would be that she's settling in somewhere for the night."

"That would be good." There was a slight lift of the
needle on the meter and Brooke held her breath. There
it was again. "I've got a faint signal again."

"I thought she might be heading toward the ocean."

"Why is that?"

"I don't know. She just likes to head west." He was
smiling to himself. He must have known she was expecting some profound reason the bird would be heading toward the sea.

"It's getting a little stronger." The needle was lifting
a little higher and Brooke felt her hope rising with it.

"You must be good luck. I have to admit I didn't
expect to find a signal at all. I lost her signal so
quickly I thought maybe she decided to migrate on
me."

"Migrate? Why would she migrate?"

"Well, it's the right time of year. Sometimes nature
yells louder than a falconer does. Or maybe it's just
that she speaks more sweetly. Either way, the bird isn't
always going to do what you want it to."

"Doesn't that drive you crazy?"

"Sometimes." He laughed. "But it's almost always

your own fault when you lose them. We're spoiled now. Falconers never used to have telemetry and I think they were a lot more careful in those days. There are days when you pick her up and look into her eyes and you know. You know that before you even weigh her if you take her into the field to fly you're going to lose her. You have to really listen."

"I wish someone would listen to me like that." She was sure she said it loud enough for him to hear her, but he looked at her like he hadn't quite made it out.

"How's the signal?"

"Pretty strong."

"Good. I think I have an idea where she might be." He pointed straight ahead.

"Is that downtown Los Angeles?" There was something amusing about the idea of that gorgeous creature hanging around in LA.

"Yep. And I bet she's sitting pretty on top of one of those buildings." Sure enough, the signal was getting stronger as they got closer. "Okay. Here's what I want you to do now. Disconnect the antennae the receiver is hooked up to now and push that button above the meter." Brooke did as she was told and when she pushed the button an antennae sprung open on the top of the receiver. It made her think of the little flag unfurling from a toy pistol.

"Bang! You're dead." She started laughing and couldn't stop. "It *is* like a gun." Marshall looked over at her and gave her a stern look. That just made her laugh harder. "I don't think you should be running around in downtown LA pointing this at the buildings." He turned his stern look into a scowl and then his face broke into a smile. "Sir, put the gun down and your hands in the air." She pointed the receiver at him, both hands on the handle. He started laughing as well.

"Come on, this is serious. We might be able to actually get a visual on her before it gets too dark."

"Yes, sir. I don't have a visual on the subject, but am certain we will have her in custody shortly." With elbows bent and both hands still on the handle of the receiver, she pointed it in the direction of the buildings ahead.

"You're nuts." He shook his head and kept smiling. "Now, when the meter starts to peg, I want you to switch the setting to medium. That will show us how close we are. If we still have a signal we are probably right on top of her."

They were just getting to the buildings. "It's pegging now. I'm switching it down. . . . and we still have a signal." She suppressed the urge to cheer.

"Okay, now point the gun all the way around us, one hundred eighty degrees and let me know where the signal is the strongest." She slowly moved the angle of the receiver and watched the meter. She did it twice to be sure.

"Strongest to our left." Marshall gently turned the plane in that direction. Brooke watched as the signal started to peg again and then was suddenly gone. "I've lost her! Did she leave?" Brooke was panicking, but Marshall seemed pleased.

"That just means she's behind us now. She must be on that building right behind us. There's a pair of binoculars right behind my seat. See if you can spot her, I'll make a few passes."

"Okay." She wasn't sure what her chances were of actually seeing the bird. She had never been very good at birdwatching, but she was willing to give it a try. They had to fly around the building about ten times before she saw anything. The light was fading and Brooke was getting frustrated. Marshall flew the plane in a gentle circle around the structure, never saying a word. The man certainly did have patience. "Wait. I see something. Right on the edge of the roof. It's a bird, but it's so tiny from here. I can't tell." She pointed in the direction she had the binoculars focused and Marshall nodded.

"Okay, take the wheel in front of you for a moment while I take a look."

"What! I can't fly this plane. I don't have a license."

"It's okay. No one is going to pull us over and arrest you. Just don't hit any buildings."

"Any buildings?! Marshall, I don't think this is a good idea. I've never flown a plane."

"It's easier than driving a car. No lines to stay in between. The hard part is taking off and landing. I won't be asking you to do any 'touch and go's,' don't worry. Just turn the wheel slowly. Don't push in on it or pull out. We're at a good altitude."

"Okay, if you really think I can do it." She took a deep breath and then put both hands on the wheel in front of her. Without even a second glance at her, Marshall put the binoculars up to his eyes and searched the ledge of the building. He seemed to look forever. Brooke's heart raced as she arced the plane around the building. He was right. It wasn't difficult at all, but it was still scary. If someone had told her yesterday that today she would be flying a plane and searching for falcons, she would have laughed at them.

"Yep. That's her all right." Marshall put down the binoculars and took back the wheel. "You did a great job, Brooke. I owe you big time."

"Oh, no!"

"What?" Marshall's eyes got round with concern.

"My camera! I can't believe I didn't bring it! Look at this sunset! I was in such a hurry. I didn't even think." She groaned and put her hand to her forehead.

"Oh, is that all." Marshall turned his attention back to the view in front of the plane. "I'll take you out again sometime if you would like. Sometime when Shae is locked safely in her mews."

"That would be great. Thank you." It really might be great, too. "So what do we do now?"

"Well, we'll fly around here until it gets dark. If you just watch the signal for a bit longer, we'll be able to tell if she moves. When it gets dark, she probably won't move again. Then we'll head back. We're basically going to put her to bed."

"She'll be there in the morning?"

"Hopefully. I'll be back out here before dawn. I know exactly which building that is. I'll see if there's a security guard or someone that can get me on the roof."

"If I didn't have to work I would ask to come. I would love to see you get her back. Could you call me and let me know that you got her down?"

"Sure. Just give me your number. I'll leave you a message in the morning."

"Sounds good." Brooke watched the meter closely as the light faded. They both sat in silence, but it was a comfortable sort of silence. She wanted to ask him a thousand questions, but she couldn't bring herself to ask. She suspected that he was thinking about nothing more than that falcon tucking her head into her feathers on the rooftop. He could be abrasive, there was no doubt about that, but he took such responsibility for the well-being of that falcon. And it was very obvious how much he loved her. Brooke wondered why he had never been married. She was sure he didn't have a girlfriend. No woman would let her significant other go for an evening flight in a two-seater Cessna with a good-looking blond. Not that she thought she was a supermodel, but she was pretty. More than likely he was single.

Brooke was sure that no one had ever loved her the

way Marshall loved that bird. Certainly no one had ever given her the kind of freedom and trust he was willing to give Shae, even in a friendship. Wouldn't that be something truly amazing?

The light was disappearing and Brooke squinted to see the needle on the meter. Without a word, Marshall reached over and pushed a button that illuminated the face of the receiver. When he pulled his hand away, it gently brushed her leg. It seemed as if he had done it on purpose, but she couldn't be certain. She was certain, though, that for a moment she had forgotten to breathe. It was hard to tell over the noise of the plane, but she thought she could hear Marshall humming to himself. She wondered if it was a lullaby.

Chapter Four

Brooke called her answering machine from work no less than ten times before eleven. Just before noon she finally had a message. "She's back. Thanks for your help." That was all it said. Marshall Anthony wasn't one to waste words. It was easy to hear the exhaustion and relief despite his brevity. The man probably drove straight to LA and slept in his car beneath the falcon. She imagined him flinching at every shadow that fell through the windshield and waking to squint into the night above. He had that depth of devotion. She wondered what sort of a father he would be. A daughter would no doubt drive him mad. He had certainly been in a rush to go somewhere once the plane was in the hangar and they had both legs on the ground. He had spoken about "putting the bird to bed" so casually, but his feet kicked at the ground and his hands wouldn't stop moving. He had been desperate to get back to the falcon and Brooke had been dying to still his hands with her own and give him a kiss that would make him plant both his feet for balance. When this thought crossed her mind, Marshall met her eyes and there was a silence so thick with possibility that she could hear her heart. Then Marshall broke the spell with a nod of thanks and they said their goodbyes walking away from one another.

"Are you taking lunch or were you thinking of daydreaming instead of eating? I'll admit that's been my most successful diet."

"I don't need to lose weight." Brooke pulled her hair out of her face and pushed away from her desk. "What are you having for lunch, Carol?"

"Good girl. You don't need to lose a single pound and neither do I. I was thinking Olivia's. Are you up for it?"

"I'm not really hungry to be honest. I was thinking a salad or something."

"I see." Carol looked her over carefully and then her face relaxed into a big smile. "Who are you in love with?" Her face tightened again and she crossed her arms over her chest. "You're not engaged to that horrible boy again are you?"

"No." Brooke laughed and wondered how Jerm was doing. "I'm not in love with anyone. I just don't happen to be all that hungry."

"Who did you meet?"

"No one."

"All right. Who did you call and hang up on twenty times this morning?"

"Carol, I was calling my answering machine, but I would hardly call that a love affair."

"And you were expecting a call from?" The woman was relentless when she was on to something.

"I helped a friend find a falcon that he lost last night. He was leaving me a message to let me know that he got her back."

"You're dating a falconer?" Brooke had never seen Carol's eyes quite so round.

"No. I'm not dating anyone. How do you know about falconers?"

"Are you kidding? That famous falconer is from Mira Loma. You know, 'the Falcon and the Snowman'? He's the falconer that sold all those secrets to the Russians? He's still in prison. Treason, you know. How romantic! A falconer."

"It's not romantic." Sometimes it seemed like without saying a word she gave Carol too much information. The woman put her hands on her hips and tilted her head. Brooke had to relent. "Okay, it's romantic, but he's not really interested, trust me."

"No? You think he is. Look at you, you're absolutely glowing." Carol sounded pleased with herself and Brooke felt her face heat up into a blush. "What does he look like?"

"He's gorgeous, Carol, I mean he's so—" She stopped herself, realizing she was on the verge of gushing. It wasn't love yet, but it could get there. "I have a picture, I'll show you." She dug through her briefcase and pulled out her miniature light box and the slides she had taken. "I'm sorry, you'll have to look at it through the loupe, but you can see it well." She handed over the slide without giving a thought to her photography.

"Wow." Carol gave the slide careful consideration. She looked at it so long that Brooke began to fidget, wondering what the woman was discovering in the color and shape. "He is very handsome, Brooke. But this—" She pointed at the slide still on the lightbox. "This is a fantastic shot. It really tells a story. You should sell it. You're very talented, Brooke."

"Thank you." Brooke bowed her head. She was unprepared for the compliment and didn't know how to take it.

"Amazing. I would like to see more of your photography." Her smile faded as the phone began to ring. "It might be Bartell. I better answer it, but after this, we're on lunch." Carol answered the phone and her expression instantly changed. She scrunched her face as she held the receiver out to Brooke. "It's Jeremy. I hope this time you're going to tell him where to go."

"He's my friend, Carol, at least for now." Carol looked at her with a question in her eyes as Brooke took the phone from her, but Brooke waved her out of the room. "I'll only be a second."

"Yeah, give him my love." Carol scowled her way out of the office and Brook sighed.

"Hello?" Brooke hadn't heard a peep out of him since they had talked about Camille. She was a little curious about what was going on.

"Hi, Brooke."

"Hi." Brooke let the silence settle and waited for him to volunteer some information.

"You were right. I think I was a little jealous about your date."

"It's not really a date, Jerm." His silence told her that he wasn't convinced. "Look, I get a little jealous too sometimes. I think it's natural. If you were a girl I would be a little jealous of your relationships too. I think it's natural. You don't have to apologize."

"Natural? I suppose."

"How's Camille?" He sounded odd and she wondered why.

"I broke it off."

"For good?"

"Maybe for good. I think it's time I got my head on straight, Brooke. I need to think for a while."

"About what, Jerm?" He seemed confused and a little sad.

"I need to talk to you, Brooke. I mean *really* talk. Can I stop by tonight?"

"No, Jerm, I have plans. It will have to be some

other night." There was a long pause and she could hear Jeremy take a deep breath.

"It's that falconer, isn't it. I mean, that's okay. I just worry is all." He didn't sound worried. He sounded upset.

"No. It's not the falconer, not the one that you are thinking of anyway. It's that nice couple that I met."

"But you could cancel." He sounded a little desperate and it worried her.

"I can't cancel. I already confirmed."

"I know, I know. You keep your commitments. Are you sure you couldn't postpone it, just this once?"

"I can meet you for lunch tomorrow."

"Dinner."

"Fine. I'll meet you for dinner."

"No. We really need to talk. I don't want to sit in a restaurant. How about if I bring over a pizza to your place?" He sounded as serious as she had ever heard him and wondered what deep mystery he thought he had solved in the last few days. When Jeremy got like this it was better to keep things light.

"No anchovies this time, okay?"

"Talk about holding a grudge. I haven't put anchovies on our pizza since we were fifteen. You haven't quit reminding me since."

"That's what old friends are for, to keep you honest. Come over at seven?"

"Seven-thirty. Make sure there's Coke in the fridge, okay?"

"You know there's always Coke in the fridge unless you happened to have been over the night before." Brooke never could figure out how he could guzzle that sugary sweet stuff.

"What are you trying to say?"

"If I had saved all the money I've spent on Coke for you in my lifetime, I would be a very rich girl." Jeremy snorted at her and Brooke couldn't help but giggle. She heard someone clearing their throat and turned to see Carol in the doorway, looking impatient. "Look, Jerm. I've got to run, but I'll see you tomorrow night, all right?"

"See you then."

"Bye." She put down the receiver and tried to ignore Carol's exasperated sigh. "Carol, he's my—"

"Yes, I know. He's your friend. And I'm telling you right now that he's going to cause you problems. He'll find a way to stand between you and anyone you happen to fall in love with, even the falconer."

"Don't be ridiculous, Carol." She shook her head and gave her a disgusted look. "Let's go get some lunch. A chicken enchilada is suddenly sounding really good." She grabbed her purse and pushed her way past the older woman who was in the middle of another great sigh.

Lunch was a lighthearted meal despite Carol's disapproval of the way Brooke chose to handle her life. Then the rest of the day flew by as Brooke got more excited about having dinner with the Shannons. She called to get directions before she left and Mary sounded just as excited about dinner as Brooke was. She was especially interested in hearing about finding Shae with Marshall, but that didn't surprise Brooke in the least.

The couple lived in Moreno Valley in a quiet housing tract where the homes were nestled together and only hinted at the owner's individuality with landscaping. Brooke had expected some glaring announcement that falconers lived on the property, but the house with the address Brooke had scribbled down was easily looked over. The home disappeared into the languid ease of the neighborhood and Brooke drove past it three times. She might have driven past a few times more if Mary hadn't stepped into the driveway and waved.

"Brooke! You found the place. I'm so glad you made it." Brooke found herself in a friendly hug as soon as she stepped out of her car. Not wanting to miss out on the friendliness, the golden retriever joined in with a generous ankle licking. "Jake, leave her alone." Mary shooed the dog away and gave Brooke an open smile. "I hope that you like lasagna. I let Robbie cook and he always seems to think he's entertaining for a large group of people." She laughed. "Or maybe a small group of large people. Either way you'll be expected to take leftovers, so I hope you like it."

"I love lasagna and I brought something that should

go nicely with it." She reached for the bag lying on the passenger seat. She handed Mary the bag and smiled. "It's my favorite Brie and the bread is wonderful."

Mary looked inside the bag and smiled back. "Thank you, Brooke. Hey, let's not save it for dinner. Let's go open it now before Robbie gets free of the kitchen." She giggled like a teenage girl and Brooke agreed by giggling back. "Follow me. I have the perfect hiding place." Mary practically scampered off and Brooke chased after her, just barely getting a glimpse of the neatly decorated house.

"Where are we going?"

"Just follow me."

"Wow. This is beautiful." Mary opened the door to a sunroom that looked like a tropical paradise. The entire room appeared to be glowing in a bath of natural light. There was an impressive collection of orchids hanging in wooden baskets and tucked into mossy containers on the tabletops. A few of the containers were bursting with brightly colored sprays of flowers. "This is really amazing, Mary."

"This is my secret hideout. Robbie made it for me. We heat it in the winter. Look there." She pointed to a small golden lizard sticking to one of the windows.

"What's that?" Brooke squinted at it.

"It's an Indo-Pacific gecko. You can't have the tropics without geckos."

"You raise geckos?"

"Geckos and orchids. Smell that orchid over there." She was pointing at a stem of small graceful flowers that were speckled with a shade of deep burgundy. Skeptical, Brooke leaned over and inhaled as close to the delicate flowers as she dared. "What do you smell?"

"Well." Brooke inhaled more deeply. "It's faint, but I think they smell like chocolate?"

"Yes." Mary clapped her hands in approval of her new friend's cleverness. "It's an Oncidium called Sherry-Baby. People say they smell like chocolate. Orchids rarely smell like anything."

"Wow." Brooke smelled the flowers one more time, proud of Mary's approval. "Such beautiful flowers too."

"They're my favorites." Mary turned to a small mosaic table with a wine rack.

She pulled out two clean glasses and opened a small refrigerator. Inside was a bottle of expensive looking seltzer water. Mary opened the bottle and poured them both a glass. Handing over the glass, she blushed a little when she saw the expression on Brooke's face. "I'm well stocked in here. Everything you need for the perfect hideway."

"I can see." Brooke sliced off a wedge of the Brie and took a taste. "This really *is* lovely, isn't it?"

"Yes." Mary refilled Brooke's glass and poured herself one as well. "Take a seat, please." Mary motioned to a very comfortable-looking wicker chair and sat in a matching chair next to it.

"This is so beautiful, Mary." Brooke took another bite of cheese and smiled. "Orchids and geckos. I thought you just liked birds."

"I lived in Florida for a while and I miss it sometimes. You know, geckos in the kitchen, orchids on the porch." She looked a little wistful and though Brooke didn't really know, she thought she could relate, so she nodded. "Robbie made me this room so that I could have my own Florida, a vacation room." Brooke sighed, looking into her wineglass.

"He sounds like a wonderful guy."

"He really is." Mary had a private smile on her face and then she noticed the look on her friend's face. "Tell me about Marshall. Did he get Shae back? I can't believe I didn't ask you that right away. Poor Marshall. He's okay, right?"

"He got her back this morning. Mary, she was on a building in downtown Los Angeles! Can you believe that?"

"I can." Mary shook her head. "You never know where a falcon might go, though most falconers pretend like they always know. That's men for you though."

"I had no idea. About the falcons I mean."

"Did you help him with the telemetry?"

"Yes, it was amazing. I can't believe we found her

when she was so far away. He was really worried about her, I could tell."

"I'm sure." Mary leaned in a little closer to Brooke and spoke softly. "There's more to that man than most people see at first glance. He's got a big heart. I don't doubt that. He just hasn't learned to—"

"Well, here you are." Suddenly a large golden dog was eagerly joining the party, his ecstatic tail threatening to knock over any number of potted plants.

"Jacob, go on. You know you're not allowed in here." Mary pointed the retriever out of the room much to his chagrin, but she looked a little embarrassed.

"So I'm slaving away in the kitchen and you've already run off with the guest of honor. I figured I would find you in the clubhouse. Have you pried any good gossip out of her yet?"

"Robbie! Don't say that. What if she thinks you're serious?"

"I'm sorry, Brooke. It's not true. Mary doesn't have to pry good gossip out of anyone."

"Robert!"

"Oh boy. I'm in trouble now." He winked at Brooke and lowered his face to smile at his wife. "Would you like to bring that snack to dinner with you or have you already spoiled your appetite? It's ready."

"Yes." Mary stood up and brushed herself off. "You ready for dinner, Brooke?"

"I can't wait." Brooke took another sip of her glass to cover her smile and got up as well.

"You know, Brooke, Brie is her favorite. You should consider yourself lucky that she shared it with you."

"Oh please, Robbie. You don't appreciate gourmet food. I see no point in sharing it with you."

"And you have no appreciation for a finely crafted lasagna, but I'm going to share mine with you anyway, so let's go eat." He put his arm around his wife and motioned for Brooke to follow.

The lasagna *was* well crafted and a comfortable silence settled on the table as they ate. The table was beautifully set, but Brooke suspected that Rob was responsible for that as well. After they had put a dent in their generous portions and the food had been complimented, Mary sighed and smiled. "Marshall got Shae back this morning."

"Hmm. Well, that's good. It's tough to lose a bird." Rob didn't seem as interested in the story as Mary obviously wanted him to be.

"Brooke went out to help him find her. She got to fly in the Cessna and use the telemetry. They found Shae in downtown LA." Mary raised her eyebrows at her husband and he smiled at her.

"Well, that does sound like quite an adventure. I imagine that's not something that you've done before."

"No. I can't say I have." Brooke smiled into her glass and blushed a little.

"Most of us can't just jump into our own private plane and chase after a lost falcon. I guess that allows for a little more carelessness."

"Robbie, be nice." Mary's lips were pressed into a tight line and she kicked him under the table. Brooke saw him rubbing at his leg.

"I'm sure he's a nice guy. I just think it would be nice to own your own plane." He didn't sound very convincing and Mary was shaking her head at him. She leaned a little closer to Brooke.

"It's jealousy, Brooke. He's rich, handsome and he is free to fly his bird whenever he wants. The other falconers dislike him for that."

"Oh come on, Mary. He's arrogant and he acts like he's too good for the rest of us." Rob turned to his wife defiantly.

"He only reacts to the way everyone else treats him. He is actually a nice person. A little withdrawn maybe, but the right woman could definitely bring him out of his shell." She answered him quietly and confidently. It seemed to pique Rob's interest. She certainly had Brooke's full attention.

"I didn't realize you knew him so well, darling."

"Oh, stop." Mary laughed and reached out to touch Brooke's arm. "We've been married for five years. It's nice to hear him get jealous once in a while." Mary moved her chair closer to her husband and put her hand on his knee. "Really, I don't know him very well at all, but he saved my bird's life once and I haven't forgotten."

"Which bird?" Now Rob truly was interested.

"Sasha. It was a couple of years before I met you."

Rob relaxed and leaned back in his chair. "A pretty girl like you, of course he would help you out. I doubt he was doing it out of the goodness of his heart."

"Actually, he told me that he can't stand redheads, so I don't think that was the case at all."

"He said that to you!" Brooke sat up straight, ready to defend her new friend.

"Apparently, his mother has red hair. I don't think he meant to offend me."

"He does seem to have a way with words, doesn't he?" Brooke shook her head and smiled.

"Since both of you are apparently smitten, we may as well hear the story." Rob seemed to be over his momentary jealousy.

"I would like it hear it." Brooke rested her chin in her hands and gave Mary her full attention.

Mary let the room go silent for a moment. Then she lifted her glass and raised it at Brooke. "Sasha was my first Red-tailed hawk. She was a good bird, caught a lot of rabbits."

"Did she die?" Brooke was aware that this question was probably rude, but she didn't really want to hear a sad story.

"No, I released her after I flew her for two years.

She's out there somewhere contributing her superior genes to the gene pool."

Rob snorted and shook his head at her. "Every apprentice thinks that their first bird is the most amazing bird to ever grace the sky."

Mary dismissed him with a wave of her hand. "Well, to me she was. She was a great bird. I was out catching jackrabbits with her one afternoon. I had found what I thought might be the perfect place. It was next to a drainage ditch and we had just had a good rain. It was a decent little pond and there were rabbits all around the edge. I kicked up one rabbit after another, but she was being really picky. Just waiting for the perfect one I guess. Unfortunately, what she decided was the perfect slip was on the other side of the pond from me. I yelled at her when I realized what she was after, but she certainly wasn't going to listen to me. Red-tails can be pretty single-minded, like some other creatures that I'm fond of." She gave Rob a look, but he had missed the comment. "She knew what she was doing though, that rabbit didn't have a chance. I was jumping up and down, cheering her on when I saw that she was looking at something above her. I was hoping there was just a vulture or an airplane flying over, but what I saw was a big dark bird tucked in a dive and heading straight for her."

"A Golden?" Rob looked chilled by the thought of it.

"What's a Golden?" Brooke asked, worried about where this story was going.

"A Golden eagle. They are three times the size of a hawk and very good at catching jackrabbits. They don't mind taking food from other birds either and wouldn't think twice about eating the hawk that actually did the hunting."

"Why didn't Sasha fly off?"

"Are you kidding? Sasha, leave a meal? I could barely get near her on a kill myself. She was going to defend her rabbit and if I was going to save her life I was going to have to get there to defend her fast. Unfortunately the quickest way to her was across the pond. It was a little deeper than I thought too."

"No. It wasn't the drainage pond on Jurupa, was it?" Rob pinched his nose with his fingers and gave his wife a pleading look.

"That would be the one."

"Oh. Man." He pushed his chair a few inches away from his wife and shook his head.

"We do what we must. You've come home smelling like a rose once or twice yourself, dear one." Mary shrugged and Rob laughed.

"Well, go on. Did you get there in time?"

"Yes, what happened, Mary?" Brooke was more interested to know what happened to the bird than how Mary smelled.

"I didn't get there in time. I saw the eagle closing in as I was splashing across as quickly as I could. I waved my arms and yelled to try to get its attention. I must have been waving a little too hard, because I lost balance and fell face first into the water. I guess I should have run *around* the pond. I was halfway there when the eagle got to her. Sasha jumped back just in time to avoid the force of the eagle's dive. There was a cloud of dust around both of them from the impact. I could just make out the two of them squaring off. The eagle must have been a female, she looked huge next to Sasha, but my hawk wasn't going anywhere. No amount of screaming and flailing was going to get their attention. I just had to get there. Fortunately, it was a young bird and she wasn't quite sure what to make of Sasha and her attitude. She took a few moments to think about what to do. Then she made up her mind. She grabbed Sasha with her foot and the two of them started rolling. Neither of the birds saw me run up. I grabbed the eagle's head and she instantly reacted by letting Sasha go and footing me. I let her head go so she could see what she was grappling with. She held on to me for another moment as if she couldn't believe what she had in her talons and then panicked, escaping the scene without the tiniest bit of grace."

"Was Sasha okay?" Brooke knew the story ended well, but couldn't help but be concerned.

"I couldn't tell. Her feathers were a mess and she was bleeding from a few places on her head and her chest. She seemed stunned. I scooped her into my arms and ran to my truck."

"You didn't leave the rabbit, did you?" Rob smiled, obviously knowing the answer.

"Of course not. It was Sasha's rabbit. I certainly wasn't going to leave it. I'm a nurse. I can think straight in emergencies."

"Amazing woman, my wife."

"Yes, she is." Brooke nodded in agreement. "Is this when Marshall shows up?"

"Yep. I was coming up the hill near where I was parked and Marshall was driving by, probably looking for ducks on the pond. When he saw me it must have been obvious I had big problems. I was covered in muck and clutching my hawk to my chest. He drove right up to me and pushed open the passenger door. He didn't even think twice about how filthy I was. He just told me to get in and started driving. He asked what happened and looked horrified when I told him. He was good friends with the only avian vet in the area and took me straight to his house. It was a lucky break for me. I would have never found a decent vet on a Sunday morning. The vet looked her over and cleaned her up. He cleaned up my hand too. That eagle got me pretty good. He gave us both antibiotics and told me to keep our wounds clean and we would both be fine. Marshall drove me back to my car and dropped me off. That's when he told me about his aversion to redheads, but he also told me that I was a damn good falconer."

"He doesn't seem like that bad of a guy at all." Brooke said this to Rob who merely shrugged.

"No. Like I said, Brooke. I think it just takes a good woman to bring out his best. That's what all these falconers need." She ruffled Rob's hair.

"Sounds like I could be in for some exciting adventures on Saturday."

"You just never know what's going to happen in the field, Brooke. Nature is full of surprises."

"It sounds like Marshall Anthony is as well." Now Brooke was really looking forward to Saturday and wondered about all the possibilities of the day. She stayed talking to the Shannons until a little past midnight. Although she knew she going to be tired and probably have a headache, it was well worth it. It had been a long time since she had found a friendship with so much promise.

Chapter Five

Brooke woke up with a headache and did her best not to sleepwalk through the day. Taking some aspirin took care of her head and a smile kept her awake. She had had a great time with the Shannons and kept daydreaming about the possibilities of Saturday with Marshall. She almost forgot that she had a date with Jeremy. It wasn't until she stopped to pick up a few groceries at the store on the way home that she remembered. Walking by the soda, it occurred to her that there wasn't any in her refrigerator. "Oh, no." She looked at her watch. If she left now, she would have just enough time to have a shower before he showed up.

Racing through the store with a case of Coke and cursing red lights on the way home, she wondered about the strange phone conversation with Jeremy. He sounded like there was definitely something going on in his head. It was a similar conversation to the one that led up to the breakup of their engagement. They thought that they were in love just because they got along so well, but there had always been something missing. Jeremy had been the first one to admit it. Brooke felt the same, but it stung a little that he had been the one to say it first. She hoped that this time he wasn't going to put an end to their friendship as well.

As soon as she let herself into her apartment, she pulled Marshall's phone number off of the refrigerator and picked up the phone. There was no time to be nervous. She needed to touch base with Marshall and find out where to meet him in the morning. Jeremy would be showing up any minute. Before she had time to think about it twice she had already dialed the number and the phone was ringing. Brooke tucked her hair behind her ears and stood up straight, already putting a smile into her words. Marshall's voicemail picked up and she frowned. She would have to leave a message. She left her phone number and asked him to call with directions and set down the phone. A glance at her watch told her she had just enough time to jump in and out of the shower.

Jeremy arrived right on time. There were a lot of things about Jerm that led people to say he was flaky, but punctuality wasn't one of them. Jeremy had never been late to anything in his life. She opened the door and gave him a hug, inviting him in. When she did, she noticed he smelled nice. She couldn't recall him ever wearing cologne before.

"You smell nice." She looked at him with a question in her eyes, but he shrugged it off.

"I took a shower. Looks like you did too, or did you try to drown yourself?"

"You know I hate to use a hairdryer, Jerm."

"I know, I've spent many a night waiting for your hair to dry so that we could go out."

"That was *once* and it was freezing outside. We aren't going anywhere tonight, so it really isn't a problem. Hey! Where's the pizza?"

"Oh, yeah, the pizza. I guess I got distracted. We can just call and order some. Let's sit down and talk for a bit first."

"Okay." Brooke squinted and looked him over carefully. Something was up, but she couldn't figure it out. She grabbed a Coke from the refrigerator and handed it to him. Then she got herself a glass of water.

"Aren't you having one?" Jeremy was already drinking his.

"No." She shook her head at him, watching him drink most of the can in a couple of swallows. "Maybe later when we eat. Let's go sit down on the couch." Jeremy nodded and they sat down together. He winced as he settled on the couch. "You okay?"

"Yeah, just a little sore." He sat silent for a moment, looking at his hands.

"Come on, Jerm. Spit it out. What's up?"

"Okay." Jeremy took a deep breath and looked at the floor. "I've been doing a lot of thinking about us and what's best for me. So I had a long talk with Camille and told her that I thought you and I should get back together."

"What!" Brooke nearly choked on the sip of water she was taking.

"I know, it's out of the blue. I've been so stupid. All this time, you were always what's best for me. I just got scared or something I guess."

"Wait!" Brooke was stunned. "Let me get this straight. You just decided that we are going to get back together?"

"Oh, no. I understand that it is going to take some time to get things back to the way they were. It's just that I'm ready to make that commitment." The phone began to ring and Brooke was relieved for the interruption.

"Hold on to that thought. It's a doozie." She got up to answer the phone, shaking her head. He was incredible. "Hello?"

"Hi, Brooke. It's Marshall. You sound upset, should I call you back later?"

"No. I'm fine."

"Are you sure? I have a strong aversion to angry women."

"No. Really, Marshall, I'm not angry. I'm . . . I'm fine." She laughed and wondered how many other aversions he had. "Let me just grab a piece of paper so that I can write down where to meet you." She reached for a pad of paper and dug through the junk drawer for a pen. "Okay, go ahead." As she began to write down directions, she glanced into the living room to see Jeremy staring dejectedly into his can of Coke. She sighed and felt her chest tighten.

"You got all that?" Marshall sounded like he was wondering what was wrong.

"I hope so. It sounds a little complicated, but I'm sure I can find it."

"Okay. I'll see you at six-thirty then."

"Six-thirty."

"Oh, and Brooke?"

"Yes?"

"Don't forget your camera." She could hear the teasing tone to his voice, but didn't feel like taking the bait.

"Goodbye, Marshall. I'll see you in the morning." She hung up the phone and turned to Jeremy. "Look, I don't think that this is the best idea. I mean, you don't really want this. It's just that you've never had to deal with me dating someone before. Not that I'm dating just yet."

"It's not that, Brooke. Think about it. We're right for each other. No one knows me better than you do. I should never have broken off our engagement."

"Now, hold on a second. I agreed to break it off. Being best friends doesn't make us soul mates. If you were a girl we wouldn't be thinking that we should be in love."

"Well, I'm not a girl."

"No, but you're pretty enough to be one." She smiled at him, but it didn't melt the severe look on his face. "Come on, Jerm. We know this won't work."

"We don't know it won't work. It didn't work three years ago, but we've grown up. I want to try again."

"Just because I'm finally dating does not mean that you're going to lose me."

"But I will. I'll lose the chance I had to make you my wife."

"You don't want me to be your wife!" Brooke felt her heart beating faster with her frustration and Jeremy gave her a pleading look.

"Brooke, remember when we were twenty-two and we got in that car accident?"

"Yes." How could she forget the car accident? It was her first introduction to being mortal. They only had a few broken bones and a lot of bruises, but they both realized at the same time that they could have lost each other forever. When Jeremy had hobbled into her hospital room and asked her to marry him, she had meant it when she said yes. "I remember." She felt her frustration leaving and the confusion setting in again.

"Please." He reached out and pulled her against

him. "Give it some thought. I just realized again that you could slip out of my life. I understand now why you didn't like Camille."

"It's not that—" Her thought was wiped away as he kissed her lips gently and stroked her hair away from her face.

"Think about it." He pulled away and looked in her eyes to smile.

"I will, but, I just don't think—"

"I'll give you some time." He turned and left her in stunned silence, shutting the door gently behind him.

Brooke didn't know what to think and wasn't sure that all the time in the world would help. She wished that she knew Camille's phone number so that she could call her and give him back. Instead, she popped "Casablanca" into the DVD player and went to sleep on the couch.

She found her way to bed sometime in the middle of the night. Her alarm woke her up at 5:00 and she rose to get ready. She made sure that she had plenty of film and all her gear was packed. After hearing Mary's story she knew to throw on her grubbiest jeans and a baseball cap. She examined herself in the mirror and thought that she didn't look half-bad, considering her choice of wardrobe. Satisfied, she loaded her car and followed the directions to meet Marshall.

It was amazing that she found the field to meet him at. She drove through acres of farmland, making turns on roads that didn't have signs. At last, she saw his Suburban parked at the edge of a field that looked just like the last fifty acres she had seen. Something made this one ideal, because Marshall stood with binoculars, intent on whatever he could see in the distance. She glanced at her watch and was relieved to see she had ten minutes to spare. She pulled up behind him, giving him room to get into the back of his truck. He never pulled his eyes from the binoculars, but she was certain he knew she was there.

When she got out of her car, Marshall waved her over and handed her the binoculars. She took them from him and held them in the direction she thought he had been looking. She could see a small pond. "There are three ducks out there, Green-winged teal. Can you see them?" Marshall was talking very softly, so Brooke just nodded in reply. How he could tell what kind of ducks they were, she had no idea. "Okay, here's what we're going to do. We'll walk out a short ways. I'll put Shae up and we'll move a little closer. When I say 'go,' you and I will run at the pond and chase the ducks off. Got it?" Brooke nodded again. Marshall looked her up and down. "Good. You're dressed for this." And from the look her gave her, he thought she looked good too. Brooke felt herself flushing under his gaze. "Okay, let's do it."

Marshall opened the back of the Suburban and prepared Shae. "Where's your camera?"

"I would like to just watch this first time. Get a feel for it."

"All right, but if she gets a duck then we are done for the day."

"I have to know what I'm taking shots of, before I start taking photos." Thinking her time spent with Marshall could be over very quickly, she tried to keep the disappointment out of her voice.

"Okay. Follow me and walk on my right. You should always walk on the opposite side of the bird in the field."

"Oh." Brooke had no idea that there was etiquette involved, but she wasn't surprised.

"Stop here." They had walked a short distance and Marshall took the hood off of Shae's head. He lifted her up to feel the wind and she pumped her wings as if to measure it. Like Brooke had seen before, the two seemed to share a moment and then Shae lifted from his glove. "Now, we'll give her some time to ring up. When those ducks see her, they won't budge. That's where you and I come in. We have to convince them to leave the pond with a peregrine above them." The way he said this implied that it was no simple task. Brooke watched as the peregrine made steady progress, mounting the sky. Her heart was racing a little. It would be a shame to end the day early, but Brooke really wanted Shae to catch a duck. As Shae became harder and harder to make out in the sky, Brooke could feel Marshall tensing at her side. He was compressing energy into his legs, getting ready to sprint. "Are you ready?"

"I'm ready."

"I'll take the right side of the lake. You take the left. Go!" Then he was gone. Surprised, Brooke started running a few seconds after him. Without a thought to being self-conscious, she chased after him, following his lead by waving her arms and yelling.

The ducks took a moment to assess the two imminent forms of danger and then they took to the air. It was only for a moment, though. They took refuge on the other side of the pond, refusing to commit to leaving the water. Brooke had just reached the water's edge and Marshall yelled to get her attention. "Stay there, Brooke. I'm going to bump them over to you. Then you try to get them up."

"Got it!" Brooke took a couple of steps back and watched Marshall racing around the pond looking every bit like a madman.

"Here they come!" The three ducks must have thought the same. They rose from their side of the pond and headed in Brooke's direction. She could tell their flight was dipping down, preparing them to ditch back into the water. Determined not to let them, Brooke flailed her arms, yelling and jumping. Then she got a little too close to the edge of the water and slipped right in. Two of the ducks skidded into water nearby. However, the impressive splash she made con-

vinced one of the ducks to abandon the idea of landing
and he took his chances in the air.

Already soaked, Brooke stayed in the position she
had landed and watched the rest of the drama unfold.
Marshall was yelling to Shae, who had already eval-
uated the situation and needed no instructions. She
was tucked into a dive that held an amazing amount
of speed and commitment. It was far more breathtak-
ing than what Brooke had seen at the Sky Trials. This
wasn't practice. This was living to see tomorrow, her
only chance at a meal. The duck didn't look nearly as
committed and in a flurry of feathers and impact, the
teal was swept from the sky.

"Wow." Brooke realized that she was still bathing
in the murky pond as Marshall reached out a hand to
help her up. He was beaming with pride.

"You can come hunting with me, anytime. You are
a first-class duck-flusher. You didn't have to go in,
though. We could have gone to another pond." He was
looking her over with a huge smile.

"Well, life is no fun if you can't get dirty." She
rubbed at her cheek and laughed, surprised at her own
lack of embarrassment.

"You must be having a fantastic time, then."

"Indeed I am." Brooke inspected the state of her
grubbiest jeans and was certain that they had never
been grubbier. Then she started laughing.

"I thought you said that life wasn't a dress rehearsal." Marshall was restraining his own laughter.

He was probably worried about embarrassing her further.

"Don't you think I dressed the part?" She did a quick turn, modeling for him. That did it. Marshall was laughing so hard he had to clutch at his stomach.

"You look incredible." He reached out a hand to her. "Come on, Brooke, let's go help out Shae."

"Oh, I'm sorry. I wasn't thinking."

"No, don't worry. I'm certain she's fine. That was the cleanest hunt I've ever seen. We just better get to her before she eats so much she bursts." He took her hand for just a moment to lead her in the right direction. Then he took it away again, wiping it on his jeans with a fresh burst of laughter. "Maybe we can find a sprinkler to rinse you off in as well." Brooke just blinked, concentrating on the warmth he left in her hand.

Shae was positioned over her quarry, a small bulge in her chest indicating how much she had already eaten. Her delicate wings were stretched across her prize as though she could guard it from any possibility of strong-arming or theft. So graceful in the air, the regal creature now consumed her meal with a ferocity that amazed Brooke. It reminded her that the bird was truly wild. Marshall hadn't tamed Shae. They had just come to an agreement.

"What are those?" Brooke pointed at two slender lengths of leather that hung loose in Marshall's hand as he slowly approached his bird.

"These are jesses. I'm going to slip them through those grommets in her anklets so that I can hold on to her. Once she's got a crop full of food she's not so interested in hanging out with me anymore."

"I know some women like that. Feed them a nice dinner and then they are done with you." Brooke meant this to be funny, but the smile had left Marshall's face. He met her eyes and she thought they seemed sad. Then his smile returned.

"You don't strike me as that sort of person, though."

"Are you kidding? One good meal makes me your friend for life."

"So if I take you out to dinner three or four times, what would that make you? My wife?" Marshall's face was blank and Brooke felt the blood draining from hers.

"Um . . ."

"How about we start with breakfast and see where it goes from there?" His expression was still unreadable, but his eyes were searching her face for something.

"Yeah, breakfast sounds nice." She wondered if he could hear the tremble in her voice and tried to mask it with a laugh. "I don't know that many places would let me in looking like this though." She raised her arms to show off the muck on her clothes and shrugged.

"No. You're probably right. I don't know that you want to climb into that spotless car of yours with those clothes either. I'll tell you what. I don't live far from here. We can go in my car and stop by my place so you can clean up. I'm sure that I have something you can wear."

"Okay." Brooke agreed right away, but she was trying not to think about wearing Marshall's clothes.

Shae was left to her meal until she had so much to eat that she was willing to step right off of it. Then Marshall tucked her into the back of his Suburban and tucked Brooke into the passenger seat, insisting she wear her seatbelt. Brooke was nervous about the possibilities of the day, but found that as more time passed she felt more and more comfortable with Marshall.

The drive was silent, but Brooke found she would rather not talk. She watched the scenery and made excuses to look at things that allowed her long glances in Marshall's direction. Her initial impression still held. He was a very handsome man, but the more she looked the more certain she was of that. He obviously had not shaved before he left that morning and the shadow that outlined his face gave it more depth than she had seen when she met him. Now the perfection of his cheekbones and the symmetry of his jaw were obvious. The lines of his expressions were graceful and dangerous, his features chiseled as deftly as the peregrine's. He must be close to six feet tall, because he stood well above Brooke's 5'8" frame. Yet she noticed that he moved with more ease than she usually noticed in men at that height. She preferred shorter men. To her it seemed that tall men were awkward. It was as though most of them woke up one morning and found that their bodies had stretched an entire foot. In their surprise, they never mastered the use of it. Perhaps Marshall had always been tall or maybe the peregrine taught him how to find ease in movement. Either way, she was certain he would never step on her feet if she danced with him. And if she danced with him, she would never be able to stop looking into his eyes. There was humor and wit in those eyes. She had never seen eyes quite that shade of green, or eyes that flashed so obviously with a thought or a new emotion. A woman could spend a lifetime interpreting those eyes and never get bored with the effort.

"Here we are." Marshall was pulling onto a dirt driveway with a sign that read "private drive." Brooke understood why soon enough, for although Marshall announced their arrival, they still had a way to go before the house appeared. It was a very small house, a neat little Spanish hacienda, not what she was expecting. As she got out of the car she looked around and noticed that the landscaping was minimal. It didn't look like he was rich at all.

"Not where you thought I'd live, huh?" His eyes were blazing with what she was certain was anger and distaste. It was the distaste that fueled her own anger. "I suppose you heard that I was rich."

"It's very nice, actually." She said it carefully, hoping he would hear her sincerity.

"But not where a rich man might live. Which is what you were expecting. Or were you hoping for that?" He faced her with his chin lifted and his eyes still sparkling with emotion. She narrowed her eyes and matched his stance.

"If you want to know what I've heard about you, Marshall Anthony, I would be happy to tell you. Yes, I have heard that you are from a rich family. I heard that you fly falcons not as a hobby, but as a way of life, because you can afford to. I've heard that you are arrogant and turn up your nose at other falconers. But it's the one thing that Mary told me I believe. I believe it because I know it from my own experience. It's that you are capable of being compassionate and deeper than most people I know. That is what makes you worth knowing better and taking a chance with. I don't care about money." She felt her eyes tearing up and turned away from him. "You can take me back to my car. I'm really not hungry."

"Mary told you that?"

"Not in so many words, but she told me the story about how you rescued her and her hawk. I thought it was a wonderful story. I thought you were someone I would like to know better." She scrubbed at the tears floating under her lashes, angry with herself for getting so emotional so quickly.

"I'm no knight in shining armor."

"No, but you try to be and really that's all that matters."

"I'm sorry." He touched her shoulder and gave it a gentle pull so that she would face him. "I think the worst sometimes when I shouldn't. My mother taught me to do that. Come on, let's get you cleaned up and feed you. I'll tell you all about my mother over breakfast. Maybe you'll hate her just as much as I do." He wiggled his eyebrows at her and she smiled. She didn't really approve of the idea of anyone hating his own mother, but she was intrigued, so she cut him some slack. Then he put his arm around her shoulder, leading her to the door. Up against his body, she felt all her anger dissipate into his warmth and approval. He was completely forgiven.

Chapter Six

Marshall's house was a mess, but in an organized sort of way. It was a maze of piles where everything seemed to have a place. The art on the walls and the carpet were pretty ordinary, but the furniture was beautiful. The house seemed decorated in every shade of wood. Every table and shelf looked unique. Without giving her a tour, he showed her where she could take a shower, giving her towels, clothes and a gentle smile. She found the bathroom was spotless, trimmed in shades of green. When Brooke pressed the towels to her nose, they smelled like fabric softener. She sighed, knowing that she could comfortably get cleaned up.

She took her time under the spray of water. It tasted like it was drawn from a well and rinsed from her hair in a soft cascade. She stayed under the warmth and sweet-smelling steam long enough to believe she had washed away any hard feelings that had risen up between her and Marshall. Then she dried off and slipped on the clothes that Marshall had left for her. They were a pair of gray sweats and a simple gray T-shirt. Both felt soft next to her skin, obviously clothes that had been worn enough times to reach the status of "favorites." At least, she thought they could be her favorite clothes.

When she stepped out of the bathroom, she could smell food cooking and found her way into the kitchen. "Hey, what's going on in here?"

"Well, I was hungry and thought we could eat sooner if I just cooked something up for the two of us."

"Okay." Brooke looked around suspiciously. "What are you cooking?"

"Bacon, eggs and toast. I have orange juice too, if you would like some of that."

"That sounds safe enough." Brooke continued to examine the kitchen, looking for a coffeepot. "What about coffee?"

"Actually, I don't drink coffee. It tastes terrible." Brooke must have looked a little stricken, because he set down his stirring spoon and reached for a cupboard door. "I think I have some instant coffee if you really want some."

"No, orange juice would be fine."

"There's glasses right next to the sink and the juice is in the refrigerator. Help yourself. Then have a seat at the table. This is just about done."

"Thank you." Brooke did as he suggested, enjoying the opportunity to watch him as he scrambled eggs and turned bacon. He certainly didn't cook with the ease of someone who had been doing it his whole life. The kitchen remained quiet except for the popping and sizzling on the stove. He invested a great deal of concentration on manipulating the food frying in the pans, but was obviously enjoying himself.

"Here you go." He sounded very proud as he slipped her plate of food on the table. So her smile only got bigger as she inspected the feast before her. The eggs were runny, the bacon overcooked, but the toast looked perfect. She was impressed that he had made this effort for her.

"It looks wonderful, Marshall. I'm starving." She *was* starving, so it tasted wonderful too. She was finished before Marshall had a chance to get halfway through his own plate. His face told her that she couldn't have given him a better compliment. He dished her up seconds without even asking.

"I don't cook often. I grew up in a house where I never really had to."

"Oh? Most men don't have to cook much growing up." She slipped another forkful of eggs in her mouth and turned her attention to her plate. She assumed that this meant Marshall's family had a cook, but she was afraid to ask.

"My mother more or less cut me off and kicked me out. I still haven't really gotten a knack for taking care of myself, but I'm working on it." He sounded embarrassed, but more because he was still mastering being on his own, than by being disowned.

"What awful thing did you do?" Brooke met his eyes this time, surprised that he was suddenly sharing so much information.

"I refused to work in the family business."

"Your mother didn't approve of you flying falcons as a career?" Brooke had kept the sarcasm out her voice. She was genuinely interested in the answer, but it was instantly obvious that she had said the wrong thing.

"No, that's not it at all." Marshall sat silent for a few more bites of food, leaving Brooke to think the conversation was over. Then he set his fork down and continued. "Actually, falcons are only one of my passions. What I wanted to be was a carpenter. Not simply, a carpenter, mind you, but an artist. I love to build furniture." He had the expression of someone who had unburdened himself of some great secret.

"All these pieces in your house are yours, aren't they?" Brooke was excited with this bit of information and was hoping for more.

"Yes, they are."

"They're gorgeous. I noticed your furniture right away."

"Thank you." It looked like Marshall might be blushing, but his tanned face hid it well. "My mother doesn't think it's so wonderful. Her father was a carpenter and she grew up poor."

"Was he as good as you are?"

"Not when he was young. His pieces didn't get really good until he was in his sixties, but he taught me everything I know. I started selling handcrafted furniture to my parents' friends when I was a teenager. I still do pretty well. I've won a few awards and now I have clients who special-order pieces from around the country."

"That is so amazing. Do you do anything that's ordinary?"

"I cook an ordinary breakfast."

"That's just the way I like it." Brooke pushed her empty plate away from her with sincerity. "If you're successful, why can't your mother accept your choice of careers?"

"She feels that any day I'll find myself a starving artist, down on my luck. Besides, she can't stand the fact that she has a son that won't fit in to her lifestyle."

"She's been trying to set you up with rich girls." Brooke couldn't help but laugh imagining Marshall's distaste with his mother's choice of dates.

"Yep, she started when I was twelve." Marshall

joined in with the laughter and started to clear the table.

"Twelve? That's ruthless! Boys don't even *like* girls when they're twelve."

"I don't really like girls now."

"Stop it. I shed all my cooties when I turned sixteen." Brooke got up to help him with the dishes.

"I wouldn't really call you a girl."

"What would you call me then?" Reaching to grab the same plate, they found their hands touching. Marshall looked her in the eyes, his hand lingering on hers.

"I would call you beautiful, intelligent, but certainly not a girl."

"Really?" Brooke tried to get her heart to slow down, but was having little success. "You've called me a girl before."

"I was mistaken." He moved his thumb lightly over the top of her hand for a moment and then pulled it away. "I make mistakes from time to time."

"I hope that you're not making one now." Brooke said it softly. She couldn't help but think of Jeremy.

"I'm pretty certain that I'm not." He reached over and cupped her chin in his hand, his eyes slowly taking in her features. Brooke wondered if her own eyes told the story that she was imagining. It was a story about a handsome falconer who thought she was someone truly amazing and how they lived happily ever after. He smiled and then gently pulled away.

"Don't you want to know what fortune I'm an heir to? What the family business is?"

"No," Brooke said honestly. Her voice was so even it surprised her. It should be shuddering with the intense pounding of her blood. "Your mother will probably make sure you don't see any of it. Besides, I'm impressed enough already with what you do." She told herself that she wasn't curious and when she saw the grateful expression on Marshall's face, she promised herself that she would never ask.

They finished clearing the dishes together. Marshall washed them and Brooke dried, putting dishes where he instructed. She stacked the last plate, then leaned her back against the counter, crossing her arms.

"I guess you'll be wanting to take me back to my car now."

"Do you want to leave?" Marshall ran a hand through his hair, pulling a few stray pieces off his face. With a clear view of his eyes, he offered her a smile that was pure mischief.

"I don't want to make myself a bother." She raised an eyebrow at him and shrugged.

"I'm rather enjoying your company. Do you have something planned for the afternoon?"

"No. Do you have any ideas?"

"What do you normally do on a Saturday afternoon?"

"Usually I have a date . . ." She paused to gauge his

reaction. It was slight, but she noticed it. "With some popcorn and a good movie."

"Really?" Yes, he was definitely relieved. "How is it that a beautiful girl like you has nothing better to do on a Saturday?" He seemed genuinely interested and Brooke was flattered.

"I guess . . ." She thought of Jeremy and briefly thought of telling their story. Then she heard Carol's voice telling her that Jeremy would somehow get in the way. So she thought better of it. "I guess I just haven't found the right person. Or even the person with the potential for being right."

"I'm always right." Marshall made this statement as if he often said it. And Brooke suspected he did.

"Yes, I noticed that you seem to think that." His eyes snapped back up and challenged hers. "I was only agreeing with you."

"Were you?"

"Nothing wrong with being right." Brooke took a step closer to him.

"Nothing indeed." Marshall reached out and took her hand. He gave it his full attention, but kept the distance between them. "How about if I take you to your car and we come back. We can rent a movie and relax for the afternoon. It will give you a chance to wash and dry your clothes."

"I don't know." Brooke tensed for a second, searching his face for ulterior motives. It was hard to think about anything but moving closer to him and the heat that was being generated by the touch of their hands. She wanted to get to know him better. She definitely didn't want to leave, but she was afraid they were moving too fast. Marshall must have felt her hesitation. He gave her hand a squeeze and pulled away.

"It's okay. I won't, I mean . . ." He stopped, searching for the right words. "I'm more comfortable here than anywhere." He gestured at the room around him. "Except for maybe in the field, but at a party or a restaurant? Forget it." He shrugged and looked to see if she understood what he was getting at. "I would really like to get to know you better. I think I would like you to get to know *me* too. It's not always that easy for me to let people in."

"Really?" Brooke couldn't manage to keep sarcasm out of her voice this time.

"Oh, you noticed that did you?" He chuckled softly, watching Brooke shake her head. "I spend a lot of time alone. I forget to be charming on occasion."

"It that what it is? You forget? Maybe I should stick around to help remind you." Brooke tapped her lips with her finger and nodded, making him laugh again.

"Maybe you should. I would just be more relaxed if we were in my own territory. So that's why I would like to hang out here. I won't try anything funny."

"I didn't think you would." She waved the thought off, although she *had* thought it and relaxed. "It's not going to be one of those brainless action movies, is it?"

"No. I believe in action movies with substance."

"Isn't that a contradiction?"

"So, it sounds like a plan then?"

"I guess." There was still a distance between them. Brooke moved a little closer and offered her hand. He reached out and took it. "Let's go then, but I'm serious. No action movies."

"Okay, no action movies." He grabbed a set of keys off the counter and led her in the direction of the door.

They settled on renting a drama and by the time they had left the store, Brooke had forgotten the name of it. She wouldn't get a chance to refresh her memory either, because it never made it into the VCR. They spent all afternoon talking.

"So, tell me, Brooke. It's fairly obvious that you are not making your fortune selling photographs. I mean, you have to take some in order to sell them. What *do* you do for a living?"

"Someday I will make a living with my camera. I'm certain I'll be that good someday." Marshall was nodding with her in agreement. She felt giddy with his confidence in her. "For now, I'm just a legal assistant for an attorney in Riverside."

"Only just?" Marshall's eyes were a little wider. "That seems like a very respectable job."

"Well, my parents, like yours, had different expectations for me." He shook his head, understanding. "I have a degree in political science. I was accepted to law school, but I haven't gotten around to going."

"You could be a lawyer and you're chasing around falconers with a camera instead?"

"You sound like my father."

"It's a good question though."

"I suppose it is." She sighed. "It's just that the law doesn't excite me. Taking the perfect picture does. I want to see things and I want to see them in ways that other people can't. I want to capture moments so perfect that when people see my photographs they wish they had been there with me. The law is only black and white. I would rather prove to people that their world is in color."

"Wow." He reached out and set his hand on her knee. "You really are amazing. You have passion. It is so hard to find someone who has a passion for anything."

"How can that be? You have a passion for the things that you do."

"Think about it, Brooke. How many people do you know that speak of something they do with a great deal of enthusiasm and love? Most people are just doing what they need to do to get to the next day."

"I guess not many." Brooke couldn't help but think of Jeremy, who seemed to have so little passion for life. Maybe it was just his style, but there had never been passion in their relationship either, just comfort. She thought about the kiss that he had given her before he left. And then she thought about the way her heart raced when Marshall merely touched her hand. Could Marshall be as passionate about her as he was with the other great loves in his life? That was of course, if he were to fall in love with her. She felt her face warm, embarrassed that she had even thought it.

"What are you thinking about?" Marshall was trying to get a good look at her face and Brooke blushed even more.

"What is it about a falcon?"

"What do you mean? Why do I love falcons?"

"It's more than that. You don't just love falcons. You get up at the crack of dawn most days of the week to fly one. You trust her completely, even though you know, sometimes she flies away. When she does, you get into an airplane, willing to chase her wherever, just to get her back. Most people can't have relationships with other people like that. What is it about the birds?" Brooke was fidgeting in her seat, worried that she had asked too much. Marshall sat in silence, but it seemed he was carefully thinking through his answer.

"It's the magic." He nodded, satisfied with his answer.

"Magic? What magic?" Brooke was hoping for a little more of an explanation.

"The magic." He looked up at her, surprised that she didn't understand. "There's something about birds in general. They fly. Sure you can explain it with math and physics, but it's more than that. Da Vinci said that if a man wore wings large enough, he could learn to fly, but he was wrong. There's a certain magic in it. Peregrines don't just understand the air, they can see it and they conquer it. You only have to look in their eyes to know that there are things they understand that we will never grasp. The best you can do is walk under their shadow and hope they might reveal a few of those mysteries."

"Have you deciphered any of those mysteries?" Brooke was enthralled. She began to wonder if she could fly a peregrine herself.

"No. I haven't. I keep hoping though." He paused for a moment and then sighed. "I imagine we're all just hoping for something to reveal life's great secrets. 'Hope is the thing with feathers that perches in the soul and sings the song without the words and never stops at all.' Have you heard that before?"

"That's beautiful. Who said that?" Brooke thought it sounded familiar.

"Emily Dickinson."

"You must read quite a bit."

"Not really. That's something that stuck with me from high school."

"Of course." Brooke moved a little closer to him and he put his arm around her shoulders, pulling her against him. "Everyone wants to believe there is something to hope for, I guess." She nestled into his shoulder and sighed. She had never felt such a wonderful sense of well being. How amazing would it be to stay like this forever? "Tell me about some of the furniture you've made."

"Oh, I have some great stories. People have interesting reasons for having a chest or a table built special. What would you like to hear about?"

"Do you have a favorite piece that you make?"

"Yes, actually. It's good to have something that you're known for. Like Sam Maloof, do you know of him?"

"He's the man that does the rocking chairs, right?"

"Wow. I'm surprised that you know about that."

"I read an article." She felt her face flushing again, but she was proud to have impressed him. "Sam Maloof lives right here in Southern California, doesn't he?"

"He does. Did you know that a Maloof rocking chair goes for about eighteen thousand dollars? And you have to wait several years to get it."

"You're kidding!"

"It's true. I hope when I'm in my eighties the furniture I build is considered that valuable."

"I'm sure it will be." She was sincere about that too. The furniture in the house truly was gorgeous. "So what is your specialty?"

"Chests. Since I was a boy I have always loved to build boxes to hide things away in. As I got older I started putting locks on them and then they became more and more ornate. I put carvings or veneer on them, whatever the client wanted. I've built some beautiful ones. I like to imagine that sometime in the distant future, my client's heirs will find these beautiful boxes with wonderful treasures in them."

"You build pirate chests!" Brooke clapped her hands with excitement and Marshall looked a little sheepish.

"Yeah, I guess I do."

"Isn't that just the best, when something we love as a child turns into a job when we are adults?"

"I guess it's one way to never grow up." He laughed at himself for a moment and then his face turned a little sullen. "That's another thing my mother was always asking me, 'When are you going to grow up and join us all in the real world, Marshall Lee?' I guess I never did."

"You shouldn't have to." Brooke was uncomfortable with Marshall's sudden change of moods and tried to get him back to talking about his work. "Tell me a story about one of the chests that you built. You said that clients have interesting requests."

"They do. One time I got a request for an extremely ornate and very large chest. It had all sorts of compartments inside for hiding small items, jewelry and things I imagine. I loved the idea of all the secret hiding places. I had already started building it when I finally realized that I was making a casket."

"A casket!"

"It's true. The old coot was going to take all of his treasures with him. I thought it was a great idea, but

I had to refuse. I don't want to be known as a casket artist."

"Didn't he have any heirs?"

"He did. I think that was the point." Marshall lifted both his hands and shrugged.

"When did you figure out you were making his casket?"

"He asked if he could come down and make sure the measurements were right. I told him that he certainly could, but I had his measurements right in front of me and I read them back to him. He said that they sounded right, but he needed to see if he actually fit in the box comfortably."

"If he could fit? You mean he was going to come over and get into the box?" Brooke put down her glass, laughing too hard to keep it steady. The image of the old man climbing into the box to try it on for size was too much for her to take.

"At first I was worried he was going to sleep in it, but he reassured me that he wouldn't actually be using it until after he had departed. Still, he thought it should be comfortable." Marshall had kept a serious face up to this point of the story, but Brooke had tears streaming down her face. "Are you okay?" He pulled away to give her a little room to breathe and then his expression opened into laughter as well.

"I'm fine." Brooke caught her breath and wiped her tears. "Was he angry that you wouldn't finish it?"

"No. He understood. I found him an excellent casket

maker and gave him the plans for the inner workings of the box. I was paid well for the design, but my name was left off it."

"And you have more stories like this?"

"A few more."

"Well, tell me one more."

Marshall told several stories with Brooke's urging. When she finally decided that she needed to leave, it was already dark. Though winter days pulled down the sun early, she had still spent an entire day with Marshall. He walked her to her car slowly and they stood talking for another half an hour before the conversation turned to goodbyes.

"I'll be taking out Shae on Monday morning. Would you like to come out and help me flush ducks again?"

"I would love to. I would have to leave by eight to get to work on time, but I could come out for a while. Of course, I couldn't jump in the pond again. I wouldn't have time to clean up."

"That's alright." Marshall laughed and squeezed her shoulder. "I only expect that on the first date."

"Oh. So it *was* a date." Brooke expected a witty answer, but there was a quiet moment. Then Marshall took her chin in both hands and bent down to kiss her. She had been avoiding this kiss and desperate for it all night. She had expected an awkward moment as they said goodbye. There was nothing awkward about this moment. Maybe there was magic in a falcon's wings, but they couldn't be more magical than Marshall's kiss. Suddenly there was nothing more than the heat of Marshall's skin. His kiss spoke of his need for her and promised at a thousand things that Jeremy had never even offered her. She wanted to stay for another few hours, just kissing him next to her car and under the stars. When Marshall pulled away, she had to stop herself from pulling him back to her. She wanted to breathe him in and dream about her future for a while longer. He caressed her cheek and helped her into her car. The expression on his face hinted at many more kisses that would be just the same. The look on his face helped, but it was still tough to leave him. Driving home, Brooke was sure that Da Vinci was right, a person could fly.

Chapter Seven

In Brooke's world, Sundays were normally reserved for all the mundane chores you couldn't bring yourself to do on a Saturday. There were things to clean and clothes to wash, but Brooke couldn't get off of the couch. She couldn't seem to finish up with Saturday. Her mind kept taking her back a day and returning her Marshall's to house. She spent all morning laughing at the witty things Marshall had said and remembering her own replies. It was amazing to have such easy conversation with someone. She spent the afternoon imagining what the rest of her life was going to be like.

So this was how it was when you met your soul mate. This was the knowing that people spoke of, something Brooke thought was mythology or wishful thinking. What she had heard was right, though. When you meet the right person, you just know. There's no explaining it. She didn't *want* anyone to explain it. She just wanted it to be forever. Forget about tomorrow. Forever had so much more promise. But she was thinking like a teenager. She was only a step away from writing her ideal married name on careless scraps of paper or the margins of the phonebook. So she tamed down her thoughts a bit, but still didn't get anything constructive done.

It was dark when the phone rang. Brooke glanced up at the television, realizing it was the only thing lighting the room and that she had no idea what program was on. She stumbled to the phone without giving any consideration to who it might be.

"Hello?"

"Hi, Brooke? It's Marshall."

"Marshall! Hi. Is everything okay?" She was surprised that he was calling so soon and suddenly very worried that he just wanted to tell her it was all a mistake.

"Fine. Everything is fine. I just thought . . . well, I wanted to give you an out if you needed one. You don't have to come out to fly Shae tomorrow morning if you don't want to."

"What? How could you think that?" Now Brooke was a little panicked, thinking her first assumption was right. "Did *you* change your mind? I mean, I understand. It is moving a little fast."

"I didn't change my mind." There was a pause. "You think we're moving too fast?"

"No." Brooke took a deep breath, realizing that he was just as panicked as her. "Marshall, I had a wonderful time. I haven't stopped thinking about you all day."

"Really? Hmm." He was silent again for a moment and Brooke thought that he must be relieved. "I just wanted to let you know that it was all right for you to change your mind."

"So you want me to change my mind?" Brooke's voice had become silky. Strange to barely recognize your own voice.

"No."

"Well, then?"

"I had a great time too, Brooke. You've been in my thoughts all day too." He sounded embarrassed.

"I have?" Excitement swept the silk right out of her voice.

"Yes, you have." Marshall chuckled. "You are an amazing woman, Brooke. I don't think I've ever met anyone so genuine. I think that when it comes to you, 'what you see is what you get.' It's refreshing and that's something that I have been looking for for a long time now."

"Wow. Thank you." Brooke paused to bask in the compliment, certain no one had ever said anything so nice to her. "I think you're really incredible too, Marshall. There is so much more to you than meets the eye. I love talking to you. No one has ever made me laugh like you do. I'm really looking forward to seeing you in the morning." Brooke's voice had gotten softer and she was feeling shy, wondering if she had said too much.

"Me too. Sweet dreams, gorgeous. I'll see you in the morning."

"Good night, Marshall." Brooke hung up the phone and sank to the floor, resting her head on her knees. This was too unbelievable to be true. Was it possible that he felt just as strongly as she did? There was no question in Brooke's mind anymore. She was falling in love.

She tried to sleep, but her mind was too busy. When she did nod off, her dreams were vibrant and sunny, but brief. She was relieved when the alarm finally sounded and announced the start of her new day. She was beginning to think that the night would never end.

They met in the same field. Their second meeting was a little reserved. Neither one of them was sure where to start or where the new boundaries might be. When Shae was set into the air, they were all business again. And with another successful hunt, came the ease that they had found two days before. They were fast becoming hunting partners, helping Shae a common goal. The peregrine was almost always successful when the two of them were together. Marshall commented that Shae was more serious about her job when

Brooke was around. It was obvious that they were a great team.

"Are you sleeping in here?" A harsh voice brought Brooke back to her desk at work.

"No. I was just—I was zoning out I guess." A little bit embarrassed, Brooke shuffled around a few papers on her desk.

"Being in love hasn't been very good for your sleeping habits. It's done wonders for your attitude, though." Carol had an approving smile on her face, but Brooke was still a little befuddled with having been caught dozing off.

"We fly that falcon right at dawn. There isn't much time for sleeping."

"Maybe you should go to bed earlier."

"I can't. Most nights we end up talking on the phone until midnight or so."

"Really?" Carol was shaking her head at the younger woman, but it was still obvious that she didn't disapprove at all. "You never talked to Jeremy like that."

"Jeremy." Brooke buried her forehead in her hands. She had barely thought about him in the last two weeks. Or maybe avoided thinking about him was the better explanation. He had called a few times, but she hadn't answered the phone. "I hope he's okay."

"Will you stop, already." Carol put both hands on her hips and succeeded in looking menacing. "He's just fine. You're happy now. Don't let him spoil it for you."

"You're right, of course. I can't help but worry about him, though. Someone has to."

"I'm sure he'll find someone else to worry after him in no time at all. It's good to care about people, Brooke. It isn't good to sacrifice your happiness for a friend, not even for a good one. That isn't a true friendship at all."

"I understand that, Carol, but that doesn't mean I should completely abandon him."

"You're hopeless, Brooke. I guess I'll have to just let you figure this out for yourself the hard way."

"Please do, Carol." She meant it, but she softened the words with a smile. Things were going so well with her and Marshall that she was certain there was very little that could break them apart.

"Well, I'm not so worried about Jeremy, anyway. I still think that he is more trouble than he's worth." She moved a hand as if to wave him away. "You'll figure out what's best to do, I imagine. At least you've fallen for a better guy. I've never seen you so smitten with someone before. Not that there's been many men in your life." She shook her head with what looked like disappointment. Brooke crossed her arms at her. "You may not know it yet, but I'm pretty sure that you've met Mr. Right."

"Mr. Right? How do you know that I've met him?"

"I didn't mean . . . well, it's just that you're so careful." Carol looked uncomfortable. "Well, he is, isn't he?"

"I don't know. He's exciting. He definitely makes my heart race, but is that really better than someone that I feel safe and comfortable with?" Brooke sighed and forgave Carol's assumption. She was having a hard time staying angry about anything lately. "Sometimes I think he's the man I've been waiting for my whole life. It just sounds so silly."

"I knew it!" Carol smiled and relaxed. "That's what love is about. It's not silly. When did you know for sure?"

"It was something that he said to me." Brooke hugged herself and leaned back in her chair. There were certain moments of her life that she knew would always be a part of her. The words and colors would stand clear in her mind forever. She knew while the moment unfolded that it was being captured like a photograph and hers to keep.

"Well, what did he say?" Carol pulled a chair up. Brooke's silence and faraway expression had her full attention.

"We had a hunt that didn't go so well a couple of days ago. I guess Shae wasn't very interested in breakfast. I can't say that I blame her. It was a beautiful cool morning. There was a stiff breeze that was just irresistible to her. She seemed to be having the ride of her life in the air. It was like watching an air show. I had never seen her fly like that before. Marshall wasn't too impressed, though. He couldn't get her attention. Eventually she went where the wind took her."

"You lost her?"

"Well, no. We had a signal on her, but I needed to get to work. So I had to leave him to track her down on his own. He wasn't real worried, just irritated. More at himself than her, I guess. He told me he knew that he shouldn't have flown her that morning. She was acting like she was a little too heavy.

"When I left I gave him a kiss goodbye and said, 'Good luck, gentle knight. I hope that you can rescue the fair maiden.' He chuckled and answered that she didn't need rescuing. Then he got quiet. He brushed the hair off my forehead with his fingertips and looked into my eyes. The way he looked at me was amazing. It made my heart ache, but it was such a sweet feeling that I didn't want it to go away. I was so afraid it would stop that I don't think I was even breathing. I'm sure that look meant that he loves me. Then he said, 'You know, I would slay dragons for you.' I couldn't bring myself to say anything. Isn't that all any woman wants, someone to slay dragons for her? I believe he meant it, too. That's when I was certain. He's the one."

"He really said that?" Carol was rapt, a hand at her throat and her eyes wide. "Men don't say things like that."

"Marshall says things like that."

"Girl, don't you lose him. He's a keeper." She

shook her head and fanned her face with her hand. Getting up out of her chair, she continued to shake her head. "What are you doing for lunch?"

"I'm meeting my friend Mary for lunch. Can I bring you back anything?"

"No thanks. You have a good time. Slay dragons. That is really something." Carol left the room still mumbling to herself.

Brooke was meeting Mary at Olivia's. Mary had never eaten there and it was Brooke's favorite Mexican restaurant. She was certain that Mary would fall in love with the fajitas. They had spoke on the phone briefly in the last two weeks, but hadn't had a chance to have any serious girl talk. Brooke was dying to tell her all about Marshall and she suspected that Mary wanted to hear all about him just as badly.

Brooke had finished her first fajita and was licking the last of the juices off her fingers when Mary rushed in. She looked harried and didn't spot Brooke right away, though she scanned the room several times. Brooke waved at her, but it was a few moments before she got her attention. Even in scrubs, the redhead really stood out. She had the attention of everyone in the room. People turned, wondering whose table she belonged at; a few businessmen tugged at their ties and wished it was theirs. "Over here, Mary."

"Oh, there you are. What a day!" Mary gave Brooke a big hug and hung her purse on the back of a chair.

She flopped into her seat and waved down a waitress. "One plate of those please." She pointed at Brooke's meal and gave the woman a pleading smile.

"Busy?" Brooke laughed.

"You could say that. I would say that nine months ago there were a lot of couples feeling amorous. We delivered more than our normal share of babies." Mary made a face that made Brooke laugh more. "There must have been something to encourage it, full moon or something. I don't know."

"Do you have to go back to work after this?"

"No, I'm done for the day. So I can have a couple of these if I want." She pointed at the basket of chips the waitress was setting on the table. "That was fast, thank you." The waitress set down a glass of water as as well with a nod and a wink. Mary raised her water glass. "To love, even if it does make my job a little crazy sometimes."

"To love." Their glasses clinked and Brooke sighed. To love, marriage and babies. Life was suddenly looking very different. "Are you and Rob planning on having a baby someday?"

"We're hoping." Mary gave a wistful sigh and stirred the ice around in her glass.

"I'm sorry. I shouldn't pry like that." Brooke hadn't meant to touch on a sore subject. She had been hanging out with Carol too long. She should think before she asked questions like that.

"No. It's okay, Brooke. It really isn't that big of a

deal. Besides, you're my friend. It's nice to talk about it with a good friend sometimes." She reached across the table to touch Brooke's hand. "We've been trying for two years now. We both really want to have a baby. It just hasn't happened." Mary looked so disappointed, but Brooke was flattered that she would talk to her about it.

"Have you been to the doctor or anything?"

"No. This is going to sound strange coming from a nurse, but I don't believe in going to the doctor for this sort of thing. If we're meant to get pregnant, we will." Mary took a deep breath and shrugged, putting a smile back on her face.

"I think that's a good way to look at it. Things happen for a reason, don't they?"

"Indeed they do. And speaking of things happening, tell me about you and Marshall. Come on. Spill it." She leaned across the table and tapped Brooke on the arm. "I've been waiting to hear about this for weeks."

"He's amazing, Mary."

"I knew it!" Mary squealed and regained the room's attention. "I was sure you two would really hit it off."

"Planning this all along, were you?" Brooke giggled, surprised that she wasn't irritated at Mary.

"No, I was just hoping. I love seeing good people come together. It seems that a lot of wonderful people just miss one another. I've always liked Marshall."

"He's incredible, Mary. I've never met anyone quite

like him. He's hard to get to know, but once he opens up, you find there's a wonderful person under there."

"Women love the dark and brooding type. There's a challenge and a reward in them."

"Robbie doesn't seem like the dark and brooding type at all." Brooke reached for a chip and leaned in closer.

"No, but he came with challenges of his own."

"How did you know that he was the one?"

"Oh, it took a while." She chuckled to herself. "He was quite a pest. Told me he was going to marry me a year before I finally agreed. He would have been a lot better off if he would have spent a little time convincing me and then asked. I guess I knew almost right away, but I can be a little stubborn. I wasn't willing to admit it for quite some time. He was persistent, though. He eventually won over my stubborn streak."

"Playing hard to get. Shame on you." Brooke wagged a finger at her friend, but she wasn't really serious.

"I wouldn't say that exactly. I mean if Marshall asked you to marry him now, what would you say?"

"Yes." Brooke covered her mouth, shocked by her reply. She hadn't even given herself a chance to think about it.

"Oh, Brooke that's wonderful! You must really think he's the one for you." Mary settled her chin into her hands, her eyes getting a little misty.

"Well, there's just one problem."

"What's that?"

"Jeremy. He wants to get back together. I love him. I just don't know. It's so different."

"Why does he want to get back together?"

"We decided that we should just be friends three years ago. He went on to date someone else, but I haven't. This is the first time he's had to deal with me dating another man. I think he just got jealous."

"So he doesn't really love you, he's just jealous?"

"I don't know." Brooke cradled her forehead in her hand. "He loves me, I just don't know if it's the way I would want to be loved. The way I feel about Marshall is very different than the way I feel about Jerm, but maybe it's just the newness of the relationship. I just really don't want to lose my best friend."

"Have you told Marshall about Jeremy?" Mary asked the question casually, but didn't meet Brooke's eyes.

"No, I haven't. There hasn't been a good time to talk about that sort of thing. He hasn't really talked much about his old girlfriends either."

"Yes, but I don't think that Marshall has ever been engaged before. He also tends to make his ex-girlfriends so angry that they disappear forever. I doubt he has any old flames hanging around that you might run into. Jeremy could definitely pop up somewhere though." Mary was obviously concerned, but Brooke brushed her off.

"I'll tell him eventually. I just need to get my head

sorted out first. I don't want to talk about it until I'm certain what I should do."

"But if you're really serious about him, I think you should be honest."

"You're right, of course." Brooke told herself that she would talk to him soon. "How do you know about his ex-girlfriends anyway?"

"Oh, I've seen a couple of them out flying with him over the years."

"He took them out hunting with him!" Brooke was startled by the jealousy that hitched in her chest. She knew it was unreasonable, but that didn't stop it from simmering up.

"Well, only once or twice, I think. He certainly hasn't had any hunting partners quite as serious as you." She was obviously holding back her laughter. Brooke thought her friend was trying not to laugh at her.

"I know, I shouldn't be jealous over something so silly." She felt her cheeks reddening just a tiny bit.

"No, it's not that." Mary was barely suppressing her giggles now. "It's just that once this woman showed up at the Sky Trials and chased him around the field, screaming at him for a half an hour. He had broken up with her and wasn't returning her calls. She called him names I never even heard before. She was very inventive."

"Marshall has that effect on women sometimes."

Brooke smiled and reminded herself that she had nothing to worry about.

"Indeed he does."

Their lunch together lasted almost two hours. Carol didn't seem to mind. Brooke just stayed to work a little later.

It was nearly eight when Brooke walked in the door of her apartment. She had gotten wrapped up in a complaint she was working on and decided to stay and finish it. The phone started ringing the moment she set her keys on the counter. She had a feeling in her gut before she even picked it up that it would be Jeremy. At least she would know if he was okay.

"Hello?"

"Hi. I've been calling the last few hours. I was getting a little worried."

"Hi, Jeremy. I was working late."

"I called the office."

"I don't answer the phones after five. You know that."

"I was just worried." He sighed.

"Are you okay?"

"Yeah." He didn't sound okay. "Have you thought any more about us?"

"Yes, Jeremy." Brooke took a big breath. "I don't think we should see each other unless it's as friends."

"I don't think I can be just friends."

"I don't want to lose you."

"But you have to choose. Are you in love with the falconer?"

"I think I might be." She said it very softly, but she was certain he could hear it.

"What about us though? I know that you love me."

"I do Jerm, but in a different way. You understand, don't you?"

"No actually, I don't, but I'm too tired to try to make sense of this right now."

"Are you feeling okay? You sound like you're sick."

"It's this conversation that's making me sick. I can't believe that you would choose someone else over our friendship."

"That's really harsh, Jerm. You shouldn't even be asking me to choose. Maybe if you have some time to think about it."

"I've had plenty of time to think about it. I guess you're just not who I thought you were."

"That's not—" There was a click as he hung up. "—fair." She sighed and set the phone back in the cradle. "But, I love you too Jerm." She whispered it softly and thought that he wouldn't have heard it even if she had yelled it in his ear.

Chapter Eight

Brooke gave herself a few moments to relax and let the confusion dissipate before she called to say good night to Marshall. She considered just going to bed, but she knew she would never get to sleep if Marshall didn't tuck her in. It had become a nightly ritual and it was a comfort she needed tonight. She wanted to tell him all about Jeremy. She wanted to talk about how she needed Jeremy in her life, but in a very different way. It really was time to talk about past relationships. Mary was right. Maybe Marshall could help her make sense of Jeremy and their relationship, or maybe he just wouldn't understand at all.

"Hi, Marshall."

"Hi, honey. You sound upset. What's up?" Marshall must have been able to hear the nervousness vibrating in her voice. From the tone of his voice, he was assuming she was upset with him.

"Nothing. It's just that, well." She wasn't so sure how to start the conversation. "I have this friend that I'm really confused about."

"Uh-oh. What did I do?"

"What? You didn't do anything. It's this friend of mine." She paused to try and think of what to say next and there seemed no good way to start the conversation. "I guess we'll sort it out somehow."

"Friends are sometimes more work than they're worth." Marshall sounded more relaxed, but not completely convinced.

"Sometimes. For the most part the work is worth it, I think."

"Well, I'm sure you two will straighten things out. You sure you're not upset with me?"

"No. Of course I'm not upset with you."

"Well, you sound tired, sweetheart. I think you should get some rest. You'll feel better in the morning."

"I guess so." She had really wanted to talk to him about Jeremy, but he was right about needing rest. She was exhausted, so she didn't argue.

"Sweet dreams, gorgeous." Marshall's voice was better than a warm blanket on a cold night and Brooke wrapped herself in it with a smile. "I'll see you Saturday morning, right?"

"We're flying Shae at dawn?" Brooke's words were starting to slur with the promise of sleep.

"No. Actually, I have a surprise for you. Meet me at Flabob at eight o'clock. I owe you a plane ride."

"You mean I get to sleep in this weekend? You're a doll." Brooke clicked off the light at her bedside and nestled into her pillows.

"Be sure to bring your camera. I've been told that you know how to use it, but I've yet to see what you can do with it." It was a taunt, but Brooke was drifting peacefully and ignored it.

"I've been preoccupied. Good night, Marshall. I'll call you tomorrow."

"Sleep well, sweetheart." Brooke was well asleep before she even hung up the phone.

Brooke erased Jeremy from her mind and spent most of the next day wondering where Marshall was taking her on Saturday. She called him and asked for hints. Then she tried tricking clues out of him, but he wasn't interested in giving up the tiniest piece of his plans. It was a good thing she only had a day to wait. She wasn't used to the patience that surprises required.

She met him at Flabob exactly at 8:00 on Saturday. He must have arrived earlier at the little airport because the plane was pulled out of the hangar and set to go when she arrived. Marshall looked excited; a flush to his cheeks and the smile that usually took some coaxing was fixed on his face.

"Where are we going?" Brooke demanded the answer even though she knew Marshall wasn't going to give it up.

"Where everyone wants to go, to Paradise."

"Paradise?"

"Wait, you'll see. It's a perfect day for it too."

"Okay." She didn't know where "Paradise" was, but it seemed a perfect day to find out. The sky was clear and blue, swept clean by a chilly breeze. It wouldn't be long until even that was warmed by the sun. She climbed into the plane, tucking her camera gear under her feet. "I'm ready. Let's go."

"Off we go then." The same smile was still settled on Marshall's face and it held Brooke's attention. She tried to watch where they were flying to, but it was difficult to keep her eyes off his face.

"We left pretty late. It's not like you to get such a late start."

"The airport doesn't open for landing until eight."

"So it's a private airport."

"Sort of." Marshall realized that she was fishing for hints again and wagged a finger at her. "No more questions until we get there."

"Yes, sir." Brooke giggled, but didn't ask any more questions. It was a short time before they had reached the edge of California and were gliding over the ocean. She was practically biting her tongue against the questions welling up. Where could they possibly be going? She fidgeted in her seat a little, ignoring Marshall's chuckles at her efforts to be still. She sighed and took in the sight of his handsome face for a while instead of wondering. She would have never guessed a month ago that she would be flying off to paradise with the love of her life. Marshall lifted the radio and was calling for landing clearance when Brooke lifted her eyes to the horizon and saw the island.

"Catalina Island! Is that where Paradise is?"

"Yep. That's where were going."

"I've never been to Catalina. I've heard it's great though."

"I think you might like it."

"You seem to have a pretty good handle on the things that I like." Brooke reached over and gave his arm a quick squeeze and then settled into her seat for the landing.

There was outside seating at the Runway Café and Marshall got them a table and breakfast. They watched the planes come in and marveled at the perfection of the morning. "We got lucky. Most mornings this airport is socked in with fog and no one can land. A day like this is hard to come by."

"A date like this is hard to come by." Brooke took a sip of her coffee and smiled. "The breakfast is nice, but the ones that you cook are better. So what do we do now? Rent a car?"

"First we are going to the Nature Center. Then we'll take a shuttle to Paradise. There's no rental cars here."

"Really? The island isn't really *that* small."

"No, but it is very difficult to even own a car here. There's a ten-year waiting list for one right now."

"You're kidding!"

"Nope. The island is well protected. Which means there is some great plant and animal life here, not to mention some excellent photo opportunities. So first we'll go to the Nature Center so that you know what you're looking for. Then we'll shuttle to Paradise to go on the Eco-tour."

"You are one clever man, Marshall Anthony! Let's get going then." Brooke was excited. She probably *would* get some fantastic photos. Even from the airport, she could tell the island was a jewel. She should have thought of coming here sooner.

Marshall held on to Brooke's hand as they wandered through the Nature Center, only letting go so that Brooke could take pictures of displays and labeled plants. She hoped they could serve as reference to the pictures she took out in the natural environment. There were eight species of plants that could be found nowhere else in the world and the island had its own subspecies of Channel Island fox, which she desperately hoped to capture on film. This was the sort of photography that was perfect for competitions.

"Do you think we'll see a fox? It says here that they aren't very shy." Brooke pointed at the placard and looked at Marshall hopefully.

"Absolutely. On a day like this, anything could happen." He bent down and kissed her on the forehead, then gave her shoulders a squeeze. "Come on princess, let's go find you a fox." Brooke giggled and let Marshall take her by the hand and lead her to Paradise.

They took the shuttle bus to the city. A guide met them and loaded them onto a four-wheel drive Jeep, promising a look at uninhabited beaches and back roads. He was true to his word. In a short amount of time the Jeep was slowing to a stop on a pristine beach, the guide pointing to the horizon line.

"You had mentioned on the phone that you wanted to see peregrines?" The guide had Marshall's full attention. "It's a little late in the migration, but there's been a few stragglers passing through. Our resident pair left over a month ago."

"Look there." Marshall pointed in the same direction as the guide and Brooke squinted. They both had more practice spotting than her, but soon she could make out the angular wings of what could only be a falcon. "We used to trap them on the beach."

"Really." Brooke couldn't take her eyes off the bird. It was just like watching Shae, but she knew she would never get close enough to look that bird in the eyes. "What were they like?"

"They were amazing. You could trap one in the morning and have it eating off the glove in the afternoon. We would fly them for the season and then leave them to finish their migration, if they didn't leave us first."

"You would go to jail for that now." The guide's

voice was tinged with disapproval and Brooke's eyes left the bird to see his expression. It matched his voice.

"Things are different now. Which is probably for the best."

"Definitely for the best." The guide still sounded agitated.

"Falconers did more to bring back the Peregrine falcon than anyone. If it wasn't for their dedication to the project, the Peregrine would still be an endangered species." Marshall sounded calm, but looked the guide in the eyes.

"A lot of people have said that they would have never become endangered if it wasn't for the falconers." The guide was meeting Marshall's gaze, but his words didn't have the same amount of conviction.

"Now, you know that isn't true." Marshall paused to watch the other man drop his gaze. "It does only take a few bad apples to give an entire group a reputation." The man nodded and Marshall smiled. "I'm sure you'll agree with me that it's fantastic to have them back."

"Indeed it is. It must be something else to have one fly for you. It's incredible enough to watch one from here."

They sat for a few more minutes in silence, watching the falcon work the wind above the waves. Brooke squeezed Marshall's hand and leaned her head against his shoulder, thinking there was noplace else that she would rather be.

The falcon was too far away to photograph, but the guide was able to lead them to every endemic plant on the island. He was even helpful about finding spots with the best lighting. Marshall and the guide were laughing and joking like old friends. The camaraderie put Brooke at ease and left her thinking about dinner parties and the sort of friends that she and Marshall would have together. She managed to photograph quail, ground squirrel, burrowing owls and a raven, but as it warmed into the afternoon, they had yet to see a fox.

They stopped to share a picnic lunch and a few stories. By the end of their meal, they were calling their guide, "Gobi." It was a nickname that everyone knew him by. The name came with an amusing story about a fish and had an off-color ending. Marshall explained that his first name was passed down in his family, but that none of his kin had policed the old west. Brooke admitted that her mother had imagined her growing up to be something equaling a water nymph. She had even birthed her daughter in a pool. Nourished by their meal and revived by their laughter, the three returned to the Jeep determined to find Brooke a fox.

"I'm surprised that we haven't seen any buffalo." Marshall made this statement with a shrug and Brooke began to laugh.

"Buffalo, you're kidding, right?"

"No. There's about three hundred buffalo here on the island. Although, technically, they're bison." Gobi sounded like the voice of reason, but Brooke still didn't believe it.

"Why on earth would there be buffalo here?"

"Zane Grey lived here for years. He wrote his books in a little house overlooking Paradise Bay, when he wasn't fishing, of course. Grey wrote westerns, you know. Well, they filmed a movie here based on one of the books he wrote. Brought fourteen buffalo on the island to make the setting authentic. You can guess what happened from there."

"Seriously? What a great story!" Brooke shook her head imagining buffalo on the beach when Marshall nudged her in the ribs.

"Hey, is that a buffalo?" Brooke looked to where Marshall was pointing and felt the Jeep slowing.

"It's a fox!" Brooke whispered, afraid the fox would startle, but it looked at them with disinterest as they inched closer. Slightly off the road, dappled in light, it turned a haughty expression to Brooke and practically posed for the shot. Brooke directed as Gobi slowly moved the Jeep, nearly finishing an entire roll of film. Then the fox turned as if on cue, disappearing into the undergrowth.

"Think you might have got some good ones there, Brooke." Marshall gave her shoulders a squeeze, congratulating her.

"Best buffalo photos I've ever taken." That got Gobi to laugh. "Who knows, maybe this is the start of something big for me."

"I bet it is, doll. You're going to make your parents very proud of you." Marshall pulled her next to him, beaming at her.

"They already are. They were disappointed about law school, but I think they always have been proud of me."

"Wish I could say the same about my parents." Marshall was laughing, so Brooke took a chance.

"When was the last time you talked to your mother? I bet she is proud of you. Parents forgive eventually."

"It's been a long time, but she made herself very clear." Marshall loosened his grip on Brooke and his back stiffened.

"Have you tried talking to her?" Now he had pulled away completely. Gobi had his attention on the road, pretending to have no interest in the conversation.

"I told you, she made herself clear."

"She could change her mind. Hasn't she ever called you?"

"She's calls once in while."

"But you don't talk to her?" Brooke was amazed. She had thought the woman had completely disappeared.

"It's only going to be the same tired old lecture. I don't see any reason to listen to her. I'm living my life the way I want to."

"I think you should give her a chance." Brooke said this softly, thinking it was sad that anyone should be cut off completely from their family.

"So we've been dating for several weeks and all of a sudden you know my mother better than I do?" Marshall's eyes were blazing and Brooke felt slapped. It had been more than several weeks, hadn't it? She had only been trying to reach out. She had obviously reached too far though.

"You're right, I'm sorry. I don't know anything about your family." She tried to stop her eyes from welling up, but it was too late. She turned her head away, embarrassed. "Someday I would like to know more about them, but not until you want to tell me." There was a long silence and Brooke kept her face turned away. She couldn't believe that she had managed to ruin such a perfect day. Then she felt Marshall's arm around her and as he pulled her close he nuzzled his face into her hair.

"I didn't mean to snap at you."

"It's okay." Brooke sniffed back her tears and took a deep breath.

"Someday I'll tell you all about my family." Brooke nodded and nestled against his body. "Although, I understand that what you really want to know is what the family fortune is." Brooke stiffened and then realized he was laughing. She turned and gave him a light punch on the arm.

"You're impossible."

"I know, but that's why you love me."

"No it's not." She met his eyes and held them. "I love you for other reasons." He smiled then and gave her a gentle kiss on the mouth. Brooke's heart was galloping and it left her breath uneven. She had totally forgotten about any chance of tears. He leaned closer and touched his lips to her ear.

"I love you too." He left his face buried in her hair and gently kissed her neck. She closed her eyes and let everything disappear. There was nothing but the promise of Marshall's breath and the sun on her face. He loved her. She had never been so happy or so certain. He kissed her one more time and pulled away just a bit, but it didn't break the spell. "Where are we heading now, Gobi?" He smiled at Brooke, then turned his attention forward.

"Wherever you want to go," Gobi answered cheerily. Although he couldn't have heard exactly what they had said, he was wearing a deep blush. Brooke might have thought that the moment was a dream, but she obviously had a witness.

"Gobi, let's go to the beach again, before we head back."

"As you wish, my fair water nymph." Gobi's blush was fading, but his smile was still bright. Brooke thought she was probably wearing the same expression as they made a right turn and headed for the ocean.

They were back at the airport and taxiing down the runway by four in the afternoon. Marshall and Gobi had exchanged numbers and Brooke hoped that they really would see him again. He seemed like the sort of person who could become a great friend. Marshall's world had opened up an extraordinary group of people to her. She felt really fortunate.

"So what are we doing now, Miss Brooke?"

"You mean you haven't seen enough of me yet today?"

"Never."

"Careful what you wish for." She waved a finger at him.

"You have a point there." Brooke poked him in the ribs and he laughed.

"Actually, I was thinking about inviting you over to dinner at my place and I'm not taking 'no' for an answer."

"Can you cook?" His eyes were sparkling and Brooke knew he had already agreed.

"Of course I can cook, but you may as well come over and find out for yourself."

"It's quite a drive from your place to mine."

"You can sleep on the couch if it gets too late."

"Sounds like a plan then."

"Good." Brooke had wanted to ask him over for a while now and knew that her apartment was in good shape for guests. She wasn't sure what took her so long to ask. It had been on the tip of her tongue several times and she had always changed the subject. Now she had finally asked, but the nervous flutter was still in her stomach. There was a nice bottle of wine on the kitchen counter and she could make an awesome white sauce for pasta, so it seemed there was little to worry about. She would just have to let the night take care of itself.

Marshall walked around her apartment and nodded with approval. "It's a little neater than my place."

"A little?" Brooke stirred the sauce with a chuckle.

"Okay, a lot neater."

"Your place is much better furnished than mine though." Brooke said it with a touch of regret although she thought her place was well decorated.

"Well, we should probably do something about that for you."

"Really?" Brooke put down her spoon and looked to see if Marshall was serious.

"There's a couple of pieces I've been wanting to experiment with. I've been talking to *Fine Woodworking* magazine about an article that I want to write for them. If you wouldn't mind there being pictures of your furniture in a magazine, I think this would be a good home for them when they're done."

"That would be fantastic! I could keep the magazine on the coffee table to show off my famous furniture. I would really love that, Marshall." He walked over and gave her a hug.

"Is there anything that I can help you with?"

"You can open that bottle of wine over there." She pointed at the bottle and quickly grabbed her spoon to stir. She didn't want to scald the sauce. Just then the phone rang and she sighed. "Actually, could you stir this for a moment while I get that?" She handed him the spoon and grabbed the phone.

"Hello."

"Brooke?"

"Yeah. Jonathan? Is everything okay?" Brooke felt her chest tighten. She couldn't think of any good reason why Jeremy's father would be calling her.

"Well, it looks like everything will be fine, but we had kind of a close one."

"What happened?" She looked up at Marshall, her panic rising, and saw his eyes darken.

"Jeremy's appendix burst. Apparently he's been sick with it for weeks, but refused to see a doctor."

"Oh, Jerm." Brooke cradled her forehead in her hand and thought about how he hadn't looked all that great when he had come over. She should have asked him again if he was okay, but she had been too worried about herself. Then he had sounded awful on the phone few nights before. "He's alright, though?"

"It looks like he made it through the worst of it. He's been asking for you. It would help if you came over to see him. I should have called you right away, when they admitted him, but I was a little frazzled."

"It's okay, I understand, Jonathan. Where is he?" Brooke scribbled down the hospital and room number. "I'll see you down there."

"What happened?" Marshall looked concerned and a little confused.

"My best friend is in the hospital. His appendix burst. God, Marshall, he could have died. I should have known he was sick. I could have made him go to the doctor." She pulled a chair out from the kitchen table and sat down. She was shaking a little and could feel the tears welling up in her eyes.

"Your best friend is a guy?"

"Yes. We've been friends since we were little kids, why?"

"It just seems odd is all." She thought he looked upset for a moment and then his face softened. "Look, that's not important right now. I'll drive you down to see him. You are definitely too upset to be driving."

"Thank you." She wondered for just a moment if Marshall was jealous, then her thoughts were taken up with the image of Jeremy in a hospital bed. She let Marshall drape a jacket over her shoulders and lead her to his car.

She gave Marshall directions to Parkview Hospital in the car and settled into her seat. She thought about telling Marshall the whole story of Jeremy and their engagement, but Marshall didn't ask any questions and Brooke couldn't seem to organize her thoughts well enough to start the conversation. Her mind kept flashing through years of memories, all warmed with Jeremy's smile. For the second time in her life she had almost lost him forever. The drive to the hospital was silent except for the sound of Brooke sniffing back her tears.

When they arrived at the hospital, Marshall offered to wait in the car for Brooke to return. Brooke shook her head at him as he took her hand to help her out of the car. "I would like it if you were there with me. You two should probably meet at some point. I wish it was better circumstances, though."

"He'll be okay." Marshall gave her shoulders a squeeze and they went inside to find his room on the second floor.

Jeremy's father was standing outside of the door to Jeremy's room and greeted Brooke. "He's sleeping right now, but it's fine to wake him up. He keeps asking for you. It was really close, Brooke. They said a few more hours and he might not have made it. He should have come in before it burst." Jeremy's father looked exhausted. Brooke thought life had been hard enough on the poor man. It was unfair enough that he had lost his wife; he shouldn't have to worry about losing his son. She reached out and gave him a hug.

"It will be okay, Jonathan." The older man nodded and Brooke released him from her embrace, giving him a gentle squeeze on the arm.

"Sometimes I think the boy is trying to get himself killed." Jonathan sighed and opened the door for Brooke. "You give him a piece of your mind. He needs to take better care of himself and he certainly won't listen to me."

"Okay." Brooked smiled at him and glanced back at Marshall. With his shoulders hunched and his lips pressed in a thin line, it was obvious that he was very uncomfortable. "Jonathan, this is my friend Marshall Anthony." The two men nodded at each other. "Will you come in with me, Marshall?" He looked as if he didn't want to, but he followed her just the same.

Brooke gasped when she saw her best friend. He looked terrible, like a mosaic of old bruises. The delicate skin under his eyes was as dark as she had ever seen it, his skin yellow and waxy looking. If she had seen him earlier, she would have known he was really sick. She should have known from the sound of his voice on the phone. "Jerm?" His eyelids fluttered.

"Brooke?" His voice was soft and raspy.

"Hi, honey." She went to the bedside and took his hand, wincing when she saw the IV.

"Where have you been?"

"I'm sorry, Jerm. I didn't know. I got here as quick as I could." She fought back fresh tears and brushed the hair off his forehead. He felt so cold.

"Could have died."

"No. If you did, I would have killed you."

"Old joke." He managed the start of a smile.

"Best I could do under the circumstances."

"Have you thought more?" He swallowed dryly and Brooke looked around for a glass of water.

"About what?" She saw a paper cup on his bedside table and reached for it.

"About getting married." Some of the water sloshed

out of the cup and Brooke steadied it. She brought it carefully to his mouth and let him take a sip.

"Jerm, I—"

"Brooke, life is so short. I don't want to live without you." The darkness below his eyes brought out their blue color and gave them a fevered intensity. "I love you."

"I know. I love you too." She stroked his cheek and stopped fighting the tears behind her eyes. They were racing down her face and burning her cheeks. "I don't want to lose you, Jerm. Why didn't you tell me you were sick? What if you had died? How could you do that to me?" She let her head fall on his chest and sobbed quietly. Behind her she heard the soft click of a door shutting and raised her head again. She rubbed her face dry and looked in the corner where Marshall had been standing, but he was gone.

"Was that the falconer?"

"Yes, that was." She felt a fresh bout of tears tighten her throat.

"Handsome."

"Yes, gorgeous." She stood up and gave Jeremy's arm a squeeze. "I better go catch him and explain things."

"I think he understands things just fine."

"How could he? I'm not sure that I understand things. I love him, Jerm. I love you too, but it's different. We'll sort it out. We have to." She gave her friend a sad smile and he sighed, then let his eyes fall shut. "I'll be right back and then I'll be here with you as much as I can until you get out. We'll have plenty of time to sort things out." She stood up and gave Jeremy one last glance. He was already asleep.

Pushing open the door, she looked down the hall both ways. "He's gone. Asked me if I would give you a ride home." Jonathan rubbed his face with one hand, looking thoughtful. "Seemed like a man with a broken heart if you ask me."

"Damn it."

"Not a heart you meant to break then?"

"Do you think I can catch him?"

"Not at the pace he was walking. He probably drove off by now."

"No. Not a heart I meant to break, not at all. He just got the wrong idea."

"I think it's about time you and Jeremy figured things out for good." He gave Brooke a gentle smile. "You always were more like a brother and sister."

"I know, Jonathan. We will." She had no idea how she would sort things out with Marshall, though. How could she have been so stupid? She could only imagine what he must be thinking right now. "Jerm's asleep again. I'm going to go sit with him for a while." She sighed and went back into the hospital room to think.

Chapter Nine

Brooke stayed with Jeremy until visiting hours ended. Marshall never answered his phone when she called. When she left a message that she needed to talk to him, he never called back. She woke in the morning with eyes so swollen that she had no choice but to stay in bed. Sleeping fitfully until noon, she had a dream that Marshall called to ask what had really happened and that he accepted her apology with a sense of humor. When the phone rang, she answered it hopefully, but it was only someone trying to give her a new credit card. She hung up and buried her head under her pillows for another hour. She went to visit Jeremy for several hours in the afternoon. They didn't say much to one another, just sat in sullen silence. When Brooke got home, she raced to the answering machine, but there were no messages.

She told herself she wouldn't, but when it was obviously too late for anyone to call, she dialed Marshall's home number. He didn't have an answering machine, so she let it ring seven times before she hung up. She had already said goodbye to her pride, so she dialed his cell phone next. When his voice mail picked up she took a deep breath and left a message that she had been rehearsing all day despite herself. "Hi. It's me. Look, I understand that you are probably really angry with me, but you don't have the whole story. It isn't fair to either of us to end things like this. I think we both need closure. Please call me. Let me explain my side of the story to you. I think you'll understand. Jeremy is my best friend, but he's not the love of my life. You'll probably think the whole thing is kind of funny." She forced a chuckle that sounded more like choking and took another breath. "If you're still angry with me afterward, then I'll leave you alone. Please Marshall, call me. I love you." She whispered the last of it, but he would hear it. She put the phone gently down in the cradle and stared at it. He would call now, maybe in an hour, but he would call. They would work it out.

She tried to watch TV for an hour, but mostly she watched the clock. The phone never made a sound. Maybe she hadn't heard it. Was the ringer turned down? It wasn't. The phone was working. She had picked it up several times to check the dial tone. Finally, she settled into bed with her head as close to the phone as she could get it. She barely slept and it never rang.

When she got up in the morning, one look in the mirror told her that going to work was out of the question. She hadn't called in sick in two years. When she called and told Carol what had happened to Jeremy, the woman offered up some sympathy for him for the first time in years. Carol even thought to ask if Brooke was all right as well and told her to take as much time off as she needed.

Brooke got dressed to go visit Jeremy at the hospital, but her heart wasn't really in it. She wanted to stay at home and mope. She wouldn't just show up at Marshall's house. If he didn't want to talk to her she wasn't going to force him. Not after hearing the story about his ex-girlfriend from Mary. That certainly wouldn't get her anywhere.

She tried to remember how it felt when Jeremy broke off their engagement. She was certain it was nothing compared to the pain she was feeling now. She had lost the man she was certain she should marry and there was absolutely nothing she could do about it.

When she got home later in the afternoon, the red light on her answering machine was blinking. Brooke raced to the machine to push it, her heart skipping when she heard Marshall's voice, then sinking as she listened. When the message ended she pushed play again to make sure she had heard it correctly. "Hi. This is Marshall. I think that we have closure. What I saw was pretty clear. There's no need to explain, so please don't call me again." It sounded like he had practiced his short speech before he had left the message on her machine. It seemed as if he had no emotion in his voice at all. Brooke sat on the floor, amazed that she had any tears left to cry.

When she had calmed down she called Mary, thinking that if anyone would have some good advice she would be the one to ask. Mary picked up on the first ring. It was as if she had been waiting for her call.

"Mary?"

"Brooke, what's wrong?"

"Marshall broke up with me." Brooke paused. She knew she sounded like a child and this was the sort of conversation she should be having with her mother, but she trusted Mary and continued. "Jeremy is in the hospital and we went to see him. Jerm asked me to marry him. I should have said no right away. Instead I told him that I love him and Marshall got the wrong idea. It's all a great big mess." She had wanted to have a calm, collected conversation about what she might do, but she was already crying again.

"Oh, honey. I'm sorry. Tell me *exactly* what happened." Mary was going to be a great mother someday. Her voice was soothing and full of concern. She would think of something. Brooke took a deep breath and explained the whole story. There was a long pause while Mary thought about the situation. Then she sighed.

"You're going to tell me it's my fault for not telling him about Jeremy, aren't you? I wanted to. I tried."

"No, Brooke. It's not your fault. You should have told him right away. That might have stopped this from happening. Still, you deserve to have your side of the story heard. From what I know about Marshall, he isn't going to give you the chance though." Brooke choked on the start of fresh tears. "Not right now, anyway. He's hurt, Brooke. He thinks you betrayed him. Give him some time. I bet he'll call you."

"You think so?" It was a positive thought. She could give him time.

"Yeah, I bet that's exactly what he'll do. I think he really cares about you. He'll come to his senses, but I would give him some space."

"Okay. That's what I'll do then."

"Keep your chin up, kiddo." Mary sounded upbeat and Brooke was definitely feeling a little better.

"I will. Thanks, Mary." They hung up the phone and Brooke thought she would probably get a call by the weekend. She just needed to be patient.

She got up the next morning and went to work. She didn't want to tell Carol about things, but she thought the blond sleuth would figure it out on her own anyway. She told Carol the bare minimum about what had happened, but Carol always knew the best questions to ask and got every last bit of information just the same. She agreed with Mary. It was best just to give him a little time.

Brooke tried to stay cheerful all week, but was sure everyone could tell that it was forced. It wasn't unusual for her to disappear to cover up a crying spell or make despairing comments at inappropriate times. She had decided that Marshall would call by the end of Sunday at the latest and was desperate for the week to hurry by. The week went slowly. The weekend went more slowly. Marshall never called. He didn't even call the next weekend or the next.

Brooke had given up hope that Marshall was going to call her. She had only left one more message on his cell phone, but she was embarrassed by the thought of it. She had pleaded with him to call and had rambled on about how much he meant to her. Even after that the phone never rang. It was hard to understand how he could just shut off his feelings like that. She thought she knew how his mother felt, calling and never getting a response. She had thought about sitting on his front porch and waiting for him to come home, but Brooke refused to humiliate herself like the woman that Mary had told her about. She wouldn't follow him around in public just to make sure he knew what she thought of him. Although she had a few choice words to call him of her own. Still, it sat heavy on her mind that if he came back with an honest apology she would forgive him. Some days that made her more angry than anything else. That was what she was most of the time now, angry. Rather than take it out on everyone else, she thought it was best to keep to herself.

"Okay. It's been almost three weeks now." Brooke hadn't heard Carol come into the room and she sighed without looking up from her desk. "You aren't talking to anyone including Jeremy and I think even he feels awful for you. You hardly talk to me except when you have to. You work is full of mistakes. Honestly, I'm a little worried about you." Carol sat down in a chair and pulled it up to the front of Brooke's desk.

"You need more than one person for an intervention, Carol." Brooke still hadn't looked up at the other woman.

"It's not an intervention, but I am worried about you."

"I just need time." Brooke looked up and scrubbed at the tears that were threatening to escape from her eyes.

"I know. You loved him, but if he doesn't even have the decency to let you explain things, then he doesn't deserve you."

"No. He doesn't. I tell myself that every day." She didn't want to talk about how much she was hurt anymore. Still, it was there so close to the surface of her silence, she couldn't stop it from welling up like tears.

"I was so sure he was the one. What if he was? What if there isn't ever anyone else?"

"There will be. It doesn't seem like it now, but there will be."

"I think I don't want there to be anyone else." Brooke shoved the papers she was working on away from her. She was so tired of feeling like this.

"That's your right to decide. Don't shut everyone else out though. You need your friends. You didn't even take that call from Mary yesterday. I bet you didn't return it either."

"I forgot." Carol was right though, she hadn't meant to return it.

"You should talk to her. She asked about you. She's worried. Seems like a nice girl, Mary."

"She is." Brooke rubbed away a few more tears and sat up straighter. Carol was probably right. She was trying to get better by shutting everyone else out, but maybe she should be letting everyone help her instead.

"You know that stupid saying about it being better to have loved and lost?" Brooke nodded her head. "It never feels like it's true. In a little while, when it hurts a little less, you need to look at what you got out of that relationship and hold on to that. You let the rest of it go and take the good stuff with you and move on."

"It's going to hurt a while." Brooke felt another wave of tears rising up and let them surface. Carol

stood up and came around to the other side of the desk
to give her a hug.

"I know it will, but let your friends help you
through it." Brooke nodded and cried for a few
minutes on Carol's shoulder.

"Thank you, Carol." Brooke gave her a hug and
then pulled away. "I better go fix my face."

"Try putting a smile on it while you're in there."

"I'll try." She offered a grin and Carol nodded.

"That's a start."

It was a little easier to get through the day with the
thought that it was just over and she needed to get on
with her life. Over is over. She repeated it like a man-
tra and forced herself to believe it, but she knew she
was going to keep hurting for a while. Still, the important thing was to get back on her feet.

She returned Mary's call when she got home and
Mary sounded relieved to hear from her.

"Brooke, I've been so worried about you. Are you
alright?"

"Yes and no. I miss him, Mary. I miss him every
day. I must pick up the phone a dozen times a night
to call him. It wouldn't do any good though. I know
that. I guess I just have to move on whether I want to
or not."

"I'm so sorry, honey. 'Everything for a reason, all
reasons with time,' they say. That doesn't help you

feel any better though. You sound like you're working through it."

"I am. I will. I just miss him. I really thought this was it for me."

"Things will work out the way they're supposed to for you. I'm sure everything will seem better in no time. You should come back over for dinner some night soon."

"I would really like that, Mary."

"I've got some really good news to tell you, but it can wait until another time when you're feeling better. Maybe when you come over."

"Are you, I mean . . ." Brooke stopped herself, afraid her guess might be wrong. "You can tell me. I'm desperate for some good news."

"We're pregnant." Mary said it softly, but Brooke squealed. She had guessed right.

"That's fantastic, Mary! How far along are you?"

"Just a couple of months now."

"Are you going to find out whether it's a girl or boy? No. Let me guess. You believe in it being a surprise."

"You're getting to know me pretty well." Mary giggled. "You know I like surprises and I prefer to believe things happen for a reason."

"I wish that was as easy for me to accept." Brooke sighed.

"Give it time, honey. I have bad times too. We all

do. It's easy to believe in fate when things are going well."

"Well, it sounds like you were right about the baby."

"Yep, I hoped we would get pregnant when we were meant to, but believe me, there were times when I had my doubts."

"Maybe we could talk about a baby shower when I come over for dinner."

"I would love that, Brooke. I really would." Mary was gushing. It was hard not to be infected by her enthusiasm.

"Well, that will give me something to take my mind off of things for a while. I can't wait to visit."

"I'll talk to Robbie and find out when a good night is. I'll call you tomorrow. You take care, okay, Brooke? You're so beautiful and sweet. I know everything is going to work out for you exactly the way it should."

"Thank you, Mary. Good night." She hung up the phone and smiled. It was hard not to be a little bit jealous, but Mary deserved to be happy. Brooke just needed to be patient and believe. Her life would turn out just as beautifully. In the meantime, she could enjoy her friend's happiness.

Brooke poured herself a glass of iced tea from the refrigerator and went into the living room to sit. All week she had been thinking about knights in shining armor. Marshall had said he would slay dragons for her, but at the first test of his faith, he had run away. She wanted to call him and yell that he had made her a promise and there were so many dragons left to slay. He was no knight, but now she wasn't certain that a knight was what she wanted. She *was* certain that it wasn't Jeremy that she wanted either. When he realized how miserable she was over losing Marshall he understood that she had never felt that way about him. Really, he had never been in love with Brooke either, at least, the way he had thought. He had a long talk with his father about how he had fallen in love with his mother and it sounded like a very different experience. When he was released from the hospital, he gave Brooke a kiss on the cheek, a thank-you and a lot of space.

There was a soft knock at the door and Brooke set down her glass. She walked to the door and checked through the peephole, but no one was there. Puzzled, she opened the door and looked around outside, but no one was around. Then she noticed a parcel wrapped in white paper leaning up against the wall. It looked like it could be a painting. Picking it up, she glanced around one last time and then took it inside. She unwrapped it in the hallway and gasped. It was a perfect painting of a peregrine falcon in a dive. The details were amazing and Brooke thought it could have been a photograph. Then she noticed the signature in the right bottom corner. It said simply "Jerm."

"Good for you, Jeremy. It's about time." There was

no note attached to the artwork, but Brooke knew exactly what it meant. As a teenager Jeremy had amazing potential as a painter and no one had been prouder of that fact than his mother. Jeremy stopped painting when she died and no amount of coaxing had been able to convince him to start again. Brooke wondered how he had gotten so much better without practicing, but maybe life was practice enough. The phone rang and Brooke answered it immediately. "Jeremy?"

"Yeah, it's me."

"This is incredible, Jerm. I mean honestly, I am so impressed."

"I enrolled in a class. It starts in January. I'm thinking about getting that degree in graphic design everyone was always talking to me about."

"That's wonderful. I'm really proud of you, Jerm."

"Yeah. I'm not so proud of me right now."

"It's okay. He would have found a reason to break up with me even if you hadn't given him one."

"We gave him a really good one, though. You haven't talked to him?"

"Not since that night. He never gave me a chance."

"I am so sorry, Brooke. I know you really loved him." He paused for a moment and Brooke knew that he really was sorry. "We haven't talked much in the last month. I wanted you to know that I'm trying to get things together for myself. Dad thinks I might have a problem letting people go, that I worry they are going to abandon me. I went to a support group last week for people who have lost their parents. I'm going to go back, I think. I had no idea there were people who understood exactly what I've been feeling. I know, you've told me I should go to one a thousand times. I just didn't believe that anyone could truly understand what I've gone through. Once again, I was being self-centered."

"You've been through a lot, Jerm. No one expects you to be perfect."

"No, but I'm not expected to ruin my best friend's life either."

"You didn't ruin my life." She laughed, softly.

"You miss him."

"I miss him a lot, but maybe it's time I start thinking about where I'm going with my own life."

"Have you taken pictures lately?"

"They're photographs, Jeremy. Honestly." She sighed and shook her head. "Come to think of it I do have a few rolls of film that I need to get developed. Maybe I'll do that tomorrow. Call me in a few days, okay?"

"I will, Brooke. Take care."

"You too." Brooke hung up the phone and went back to take a second look at the painting. There was no doubt that Jeremy had a lot of talent. Maybe now he was finally growing up as well. Just like they had for most of their lives, Brooke imagined that she was growing up with him.

*   *   *

Marshall drove up to the field before the sun was even hinting at warming the horizon. He hadn't seemed to need much sleep in the last few weeks, but his waking hours weren't always busy. The only time his mind was still and he felt at ease was when he was flying Shae. Even then he was very aware that they were alone. Maybe he had been a fool to think it was better to have a partner. He had always been happiest in an open field with only a peregrine's shadow for company.

It was going to be a good half an hour before it was light enough to send Shae into the sky. It seemed he found himself with more moments to think than he ever had before. Yet there were so many things that he just didn't want to think about. He couldn't seem to get any work done. He was seriously considering ditching the article he had promised to write. Just looking at the plans for the pieces that he had wanted to craft made him angry. Marshall sipped his coffee and willed the darkness to become morning. He missed her. He missed her every day, but he was better off without her.

When the sun had finally illuminated the pond enough to see shadows, Marshall crept across the field and spotted three ducks floating across the shallow water. He couldn't be certain, but he imagined they were teal. He went back to the Suburban to wait a few more moments for the dawn to take hold. It was downright chilly outside. He pulled his jacket collar closer to his face and watched the steady progress of his breath turning to steam in front of his face. This was the best time of the day, cold and still with so much promise. Everything was sleeping and Marshall was two steps ahead of the world.

Shae felt perfect on his fist. She was alert and straining to catch a glimpse of the morning through her hood. He could feel all of her speed and energy compressed and ready to be released like a tensed spring. All Marshall had to do was release her to the sky. You could tell sometimes just from the way a bird sits that it is going to be a perfect hunt.

When the hood was slipped off, Shae shared a moment with Marshall. Stretching her wings as if to test the consistency of the air, Shae surveyed the area. She seemed to recognize it as one of their favorite hunting grounds instantly. With one look to Marshall, she launched away from the glove and propelled herself up with all of the determination her tensed body had promised. She was ringing up in a tight spiral with the form and consistency expected to win the Sky Trials. Marshall stood a while to watch her with admiration.

She had nearly been swallowed by the sky when Marshall remembered to move. She was just a speck and he would lose sight of her when he walked, but he trusted she would follow as he approached the pond.

The ducks were sitting tight on the water, their eyes addressing the sky above them. This time of the year there were new ducks migrating through every day, but a peregrine silhouette was something every bird understood. Marshall glanced up, but he was uncertain where she was above him. Believing she must be in position, he raced for the water.

He had been right. They were Green-winged teal. Watching him running, two of the ducks moved calmly to the center of the water, but the third was a young drake and panicked. He exploded off of the water with deliberate wing beats that gave him more and more speed. Shae was so high that his speed wouldn't make a difference. Marshall could see her form tucked and diving, a bullet from above. She reached the drake in seconds. Marshall could hear the wind whistling across her feathers and through her bells. Normally, he would cheer her on or applaud the duck if it out-flew her, but the whole world seemed steeped in a silence he didn't want to disturb. There was nothing but the sound of Shae moving through the air.

Just as Shae was about to hit the duck, the drake veered and she missed. It looked like a move that was more luck than skill, but it saved him just the same. Shae pitched back up, preparing for another dive. She wouldn't have the force of her first attack, but she was committed to the flight. It seemed the duck would get away and Shae didn't have enough height for a reasonable dive, but she dove at him just the same. This time the drake was too rattled to veer away and Shae made contact. There was hardly any impact with such a short dive. She had done little more than give the drake a push. Realizing it was her last chance, she reached out with her talons and bound to the duck, refusing to allow his escape.

Suddenly the silence was broken and the air seemed to come alive with the sound of morning bird calls and insect wings. Marshall was shouting at Shae to let the other bird go. The drake was fighting and the peregrine's wings weren't powerful enough to hold them both aloft. They were both plummeting from the sky in a flurry of feathers. Maybe it was that birds have no fear of falling or that Shae was so single-minded that she just couldn't let go and lose what was in her grasp, but no amount of yelling separated the two. As Marshall watched, they could have been falling forever, but he was still helpless to stop them. They met the ground with a sound that Marshall felt in the depths of his stomach rather than hearing with his ears. He waited a moment for the nausea to stop rolling through his gut, then he made the slow walk to the fallen birds.

They were lying apart on the ground, a gentle breeze still ruffling the feathers on the falcon, but that was all the movement Marshall could see. The air must be a bitter mistress to make something so powerful and equally fragile. Shae had won her quarry, but it would be the last time.

Marshall tucked the duck into his game bag, surprised that he had no ill feelings toward the young teal. Nature doesn't forgive mistakes, not even for the sake of a falconry bird. Every falconer understands that the sport is bound to leave you heartbroken eventually. He scooped up his falcon and cradled her gently in his arms. Maybe it was better that Brooke hadn't been here to see this, for her own sake. For his sake, maybe it would have been better if she had been. He sat down in the close-cut stubble of the winter field and though he had lost birds before, he began to cry. Shae had been a fantastic peregrine, but it was suddenly very clear that he had lost a great deal more than his bird.

Chapter Ten

Brooke waited until she was home before she looked at the photographs she had picked up from the developer. It was unlike her not to tear through the envelopes, searching for that one perfect shot she might have taken. She was having trouble bringing herself to look at the moments captured from Paradise. She knew that was foolish. She had already experienced the range of emotions from a breakup. She wasn't going to feel anything new. Then she realized that maybe she was just afraid she wouldn't feel anything at all.

Steeling herself, she carefully opened the first envelope at the kitchen table and smiled. They were all photos of plants, but they were very well done. Gobi certainly had been helpful with finding the right light.

168

She could remember all of the names too. The first few pictures were St. Catherine's Lace and Wild Tomato. It really had been an amazing day. Opening the next envelope, she found some good landscape shots of the beach. Catalina Island was definitely a treasure. She had taken one roll of slides and saved those for last. She set up her light box and her loupe, then carefully pulled out a slide. The first two slides were disappointing. She was uncertain what she had even been trying to find in the lens. Then she came to the slides of the fox. In this group of shots, she found the one picture she had been hoping for. The sun danced across the rich fur of the fox, gently back-lighting her. She filled most of the frame, but it was her face that grabbed your attention. She had the haughty gaze of royalty and she looked you right in the eyes. Brooke gasped and then clapped her hands together. It was a perfect shot. It was also the one that she was going to enter the California Wildlife Photography Contest with. She had a certainty she had never felt before about it too. She was going to win.

Brooke thought about putting the rest of the pictures away somewhere and forgetting about them, but she knew that was the wrong thing to do. Santa Catalina Island was her island too. She had loved Paradise and didn't want to forget it. Carol had said to keep the good things; that way you kept growing. Brooke believed that for once the woman was absolutely right. So when she had her fox slide blown up into a photograph and matted, she also took in her favorite plant photos as well. She carefully framed and labeled them and used them to decorate her hallway.

Brooke had been thinking a lot about what she should be doing with the rest of her life. She knew that she wanted to be a photographer, but wondered if thinking she could change the world with art might be a little naïve. She began to do some research on her own and eventually decided to have a talk with her boss. It ended up being a long meeting and Carol nearly attacked her when it broke off so that Bartell could get to court in time.

"Well, what did he say?"

"He said I could have a raise to help pay for law school." Brooke sat down at her desk and smoothed out the wrinkles on her new shirt.

"Well, maybe I should go to law school too then."

"Maybe you should." Brooke laughed, knowing full well that Carol made a lot more money than she did.

"All that time in his office and that's all he said?"

"We just talked."

"About?

"About why I decided to go to law school."

"You're impossible. You know I'm going to just keep asking questions until you tell me everything." Brooke knew it was true, but Carol had never admitted to such a thing before. Then Brooke realized that the other woman was actually angry with her.

"Are you upset because I didn't talk to you about it first?"

"No." It was a lie. Brooke could tell by the way the line of Carol's mouth disappeared.

"Carol, I didn't talk to you because I knew I would have your support one hundred percent. I wasn't so sure about Bartell. That's why I talked to him first."

"Oh." She still looked a bit annoyed, but most of the tightness had left her face.

"I decided that I want to be an environmental attorney."

"Really?" Carol's eyes lit up and Brooke smiled.

"I actually gave the attorney for the Peregrine Fund a call and talked to him for a long time. Talking to him, I realized that if I were a practicing attorney, there is a lot I could do to help right here in California."

"And your photography? I really think you're getting quite good at that."

"Thank you." Brooke blushed a little, but took the compliment gracefully. "I think that an environmental attorney should know about the habitat and species she is helping to protect, don't you?"

"I see. Photography on 'business' trips, how clever!"

"Not only that, but I could eventually do slide shows and talks to help convince people how important it is to protect our natural resources."

"That sounds like a great plan. Where are you thinking of going to school? You had really good LSAT scores, didn't you?"

"They weren't bad. Actually, Riverside is opening up a new law school at the University this coming fall."

"It's about time. That's been in the works for years."

"Yeah, that's what Bartell said." Brooke smiled. "I talked to one of the professors and he seemed to think I had an excellent chance of getting accepted. Bartell knows the new dean as well and said he would write me a letter of recommendation."

"That's fantastic, Brooke!"

"I'm really excited. My parents are too. Mom said she knew if she was patient, I would figure out what to do with my life. Not that she wouldn't love me no matter what." Brooke shrugged.

"Well, you have had quite an interesting few months, that's for sure."

"Indeed I have."

"Nothing still from Marshall?"

"No." Brooke shook her head and looked down. She still thought about him a lot.

"Well, don't be surprised if one day he just shows up. Men do that when you least expect it."

"Not Marshall."

"Well, maybe not. Still, look at the great things you're doing now. You should be very proud of yourself."

"I haven't done anything yet, but I'll get there. Well, I've got some work to catch up on."

"Yeah, me too." Carol took the hint. She gave Brooke a warm smile and left the room. Brooke really did have a lot to do, but she took a few minutes to just sit at her desk and daydream.

Brooke hadn't had a chance to see the Shannons for weeks and was excited when the weekend arrived and she could visit them. Mary was four months pregnant now and although she wasn't showing, the glow of her pregnancy was obvious to anyone who knew her.

"Mary, you look great!" Brooke gave her a big hug and then let Mary lead the way into her house.

"What's this that you brought?" Mary pointed to the package Brooke was carrying in her hand.

"It's a painting from Jeremy. He thought he would donate it to the Hawking Club's raffle."

"Can I see it?"

"Of course!" Brooke unwrapped it carefully. She was very proud of Jeremy's work and this painting was even better than the first one he had given her.

"Wow, this is incredible. Robbie, come here! Look at the painting from Jeremy." Rob appeared from the back of the house with a smile on his face and Jake at his heels. Mary handed the painting to her husband and beamed. "It's fantastic, isn't it?"

"It looks like Mariah." Rob was squinting at the picture and his wife tilted her head at him.

"It looks like a Harris' hawk, Robbie. They all look the same."

"No, I'm serious, honey. This is your bird, look." Without touching the picture, Rob pointed out the details. "See the one feather on the top of her head? That white one that's always out of place."

Mary turned to look at Brooke and shrugged. "My bird always looks like she had 'bed-head'."

"And look there, see the scar on her cere? This is Mariah."

"You're right. It does look like her." Mary looked at Brooke, hoping for an answer.

"Jeremy stops by once in a while to beg me for photographs to paint from. That's your bird he painted. We didn't think that you would notice. Jeremy is going to paint one for you two as well, but he wants to do a better one."

"A better one? This one is fantastic." Rob shook his head in disbelief. "I can't wait to see what he paints for us."

"How's Jeremy doing?" Mary looked like she wasn't sure if she should ask.

"He's doing great! He has the sweetest girlfriend. I went to lunch with them yesterday."

"Already!" Mary looked insulted, but Brooke waved it off.

"He wasn't still in love with me. I don't think Jeremy has actually been in love for a long time. It's hard to love anyone when you're afraid that everyone will leave you."

"Sounds like you girls have some gossiping to do. I'll leave you be. I have some hoods I want to work on." Mary snorted at her husband and pointed the way to his office.

"We are not gossiping. Come on Brooke, let's go sit down on the couch." They settled into the living room and Mary turned to face her friend. "So is Jeremy still going to those group sessions?"

"Yes, he's getting a lot out of them I think. As a matter of fact, that's where he met his new girlfriend."

"That's really wonderful for him. He should have gotten support a long time ago." Mary reached out to pat Brooke's knee. "Not that you weren't a good friend to him, but it's important to talk with people who have experienced the same loss."

"I'm sure that Jerm would agree with you."

"So, what about you? Are you dating anyone?"

"No. I've been kind of busy." Brooke noticed that Mary hadn't met her eyes and got suspicious. "Why? Are you thinking of setting me up with someone?"

"No. Not at all." Mary shrugged but still hadn't looked up.

"What is it then?" Brooke bent down trying to get her friend to look at her and laughed.

"It's just . . . I know someone that's, well, that's interested in you."

"Who?"

"He's shy. I can't say." Mary looked up at her finally, but her face was just about as red as her hair.

"That's really flattering. I just don't think I'm ready yet."

"I think he might wait."

"Okay, but he may be waiting a while."

"He'll understand." Mary's face was returning to a normal color and Brooke could tell she was going to change the subject. "So, Robbie and I wanted to ask you if you would be interested in being the godmother of our baby."

"Me?"

"Yes, you." Brooke searched Mary's face, but she was obviously serious.

"But I'm not married. I don't own a house. I haven't even had brothers and sisters. I wouldn't know how to raise a child if, well, you know. Anyway, maybe you should rethink that. I mean, I'm flattered, but . . ."

"I'm very serious, Brooke. You have a bright future. I don't doubt that you're going to be a successful attorney *and* a famous photographer. That's the sort of woman I would want raising my little girl if anything happened to us."

"Girl?" Brooke gave her a suspicious look.

"I don't know for sure, of course. Call it mother's intuition."

"Can I think about it?"

"You should think about it. It's a serious commitment. I know you would be wonderful though."

"I'll let you know then." Brooke knew her answer already. She would love to be the baby's godmother.

Brooke and Mary had a few cups of herbal tea and thought up names for her new baby. They had come up with a few good ones, but mostly they came up with the most ridiculous names they could think of and enjoyed the laughs. Brooke left early so that she would get a good night's sleep and it was only five when she got home.

She hadn't been home very long when the phone rang. Expecting it to be Jeremy, she picked it up right away.

"Hello?"

"Hello. May I speak with Brooke please."

"This is Brooke."

"Hello, Brooke. This is Alicia Anthony."

"Hi, what can I do for you?" Brooke tried to be polite, but she was confused. She couldn't think of anyone she knew that was named Alicia.

"I'm Marshall's mother."

"Marshall's . . . ? Oh! Is he okay? Did something happen?"

"No honey, he's fine. I just wanted to talk to you before he did."

"He's going to talk to me?"

"Yes, he's been working up the courage all week, I think."

"So he's been talking to you as well?" Brooke could

hardly believe this. She pulled up a chair so that she could sit down.

"Yes, he started talking to me about a month ago, after his bird died."

"Shae's dead!"

"Oh dear. I wasn't supposed to tell you that. He said you would be upset when you found out. I need to learn not to say the first thing that comes to mind, it seems."

"It's okay, Mrs. Anthony. What was it you wanted to talk to me about?"

"Please. Please, darling. Call me Alicia."

"Okay, Alicia." Brooke found herself grinning. This was exactly how she had imagined his mother.

"Well, I haven't always been a very good mother to that boy, but I thought maybe I could do this one thing for him. I want to ask you for a favor."

"What is that?"

"When he comes to talk to you, just give him a chance. He knows he made a big mistake by not talking to you, just listen to him." Brooke sat for a moment in silence, more because she couldn't believe this was happening than that she didn't have an answer.

"Okay. I can promise to at least listen." Just then there was a rap on the door and Brooke jumped. "Someone's knocking on my door, Alicia. I should go."

"That's probably him. Thank you for the favor,

Brooke. I really hope you kids work things out. You sound like a wonderful girl. I would love to meet you."

"Thank you. I can't promise that, but who knows." Brooke hung up the phone and walked slowly to the door, trying to give herself time to prepare. Alicia hadn't been kidding. She opened the door and found Marshall on her doorstep.

"Hi, Brooke."

"Marshall." They stood for a moment just looking at one another. He was just as gorgeous as she remembered him. He looked like he hadn't shaved in a few days, but the shadow on his face made his eyes look a deeper shade of green. Brooke felt her breath catch and then remembered what he had put her through and stood up straighter.

"Do you have a few minutes to talk? I have a couple of things I'd like to say to you." He looked her straight in the eye and didn't flinch. He didn't look like a man who was going to apologize at all.

"Sure. Come on in." Brooke turned to her side to allow him to walk past and found that anger was pressing on her chest. How dare he think he could just walk right back into her life. She hadn't heard a peep from him in over two months. Even after she had begged, there hadn't been a word or even a postcard. She should kick him out, call him all the names she had collected just for him and yet she had promised Alicia, so she let him in. "Have a seat." She pointed him to the couch and sat in a recliner across the room.

"I'm sorry." Marshall still hadn't stopped looking at her and she hardened her gaze.

"So am I."

"Mary told me the whole story. I should have given you a chance to explain."

"Mary told you?" Brooke buried her hands in her face. She had a friend that was interested in her! Brooke was going to have to a word with that woman. "Couldn't you have just asked me?"

"I didn't think you would be willing to explain after all this time."

"So what's with the sudden change of heart?" Brooke snapped at him and crossed her arms. She was hardly going to let him back into her life just because he apologized.

"Shae died."

"I'm sorry." He looked taken aback with her lack of emotion, but he had no idea that she already knew.

"I lost more than Shae out in that field, Brooke. I lost the woman that I love. I've been an idiot. I should have given you a chance, but I was too busy hanging on to what I was certain I knew to be true and in the meantime I lost everything. I'm too narrow-minded."

"You never answered my calls. I begged you to talk to me and I never heard a thing. I lost not just the man I loved, but my pride as well!" She was yelling at him now and even through the tears she could see his eyes hadn't left her face.

"I never listened to your messages. I erased them."

"How could you? You didn't even listen to them?" She ran her fingers under her eyes and tried to get her vision to clear.

"I thought you had betrayed me. At least, I was certain you had strung me along. I mean, Brooke, I heard you tell Jeremy that you loved him. I thought you loved me." The pain in his eyes was obvious. She hadn't been the only one with her pride wounded. "I just wanted to forget you existed, but I couldn't." At last he had taken his gaze from her face and kept it on the floor. "I thought that with you I could do anything, that I could protect you from everything. I thought I could spend the rest of my life with you and yet the first opportunity I had to prove that I believed in you, I ran away."

"But now you're back."

"I've spent a lot of time thinking and I want to ask you to give me another chance."

"How do I know that you won't just run again? How do I know that the second we get in a fight you aren't going to disappear and refuse to take my calls? You broke my heart, Marshall. I can't afford to let you hurt me like that again." Marshall was nodding like he understood.

"I have something for you. Will you come with me?"

"No. I'm sorry. I can't do this." Brooke stood up and felt her face flood with tears. "You need to go." She turned her back on him and pointed to the door.

There was silence past her tears and she waited to hear the sound of the door. Then she felt a hand on her shoulder.

"Please, Brooke. I know I made a mistake, but I have never felt this way about anyone. I'm begging *you* now. Give me another chance. Come with me. Let me show you what I mean."

"Why should I?" Then she turned to look at him and saw that he was crying as well. "Oh, don't." She reached out and touched his face, but her fingers were so wet already she couldn't feel the tears. Maybe it was all the years of comforting her best friend, but without thinking, she put her arms around him and pulled him close. "It's okay. I'll look. Let's go look." They both wiped at their faces with their sleeves and smiled tentatively at one another. "I'm not promising anything, Marshall, but I'll come and look."

"Fair enough." Marshall started to take her hand, but she shook her head. "It's out here, follow me." She followed him out the door and to his Suburban, which had a trailer attached to the back. There was something in the trailer, but it was covered with blankets and tied down. "Just give me a second to uncover it." Marshall untied it carefully and then waved her closer. "I had promised you furniture for your living room. I've made those pieces I told you about for the magazine and you can have those as well. I wasn't sure if you wanted them. This I made with only you in mind and I hope you'll accept it. He pulled the blankets off and revealed a beautiful chest underneath. "It's a hope chest."

"It's beautiful." Brooke couldn't help herself. She reached out to touch the carvings in the top and the sides. The chest was adorned with carved feathers, every last one perfect.

"There's something inside as well." Marshall lifted the top to reveal a brass plate inscribed on the underside of the lid. Brooke read it to herself. It said, *Hope is the thing with feathers.* Then he reached inside and pulled out a small black velvet box. Brooke gasped.

"No, Marshall. I don't think—"

"Just listen for a second." He opened the box and showed her a diamond solitaire ring.

"It's beautiful, but I can't." It really was a beautiful ring, simple the way she liked them and in a marquis cut. The diamond seemed to throw back more light than it could have possibly taken in. "You shouldn't have."

"Will you just listen?" He almost sounded angry now and she stopped to let him finish. "Brooke, if you say that you will marry me and wear this ring then I can honestly promise you that I will never run away again." He put a finger to her lips because she was starting to protest again. "We don't have to get married tomorrow. We can be engaged for three years if you want. That ring is my promise to you that no matter what happens between us, I will always give us a chance to talk it out. I'll never disappear again."

"I don't know. I don't know what to say." Brooke was crying again, but she could feel the corners of her mouth twitching into a smile at the same time.

"Just answer me, Brooke, will you marry me?" He had taken her hand and was down on his knees. When she met those same green eyes that had stolen her heart from behind her camera lens, she knew what the answer had to be.

"Yes, Marshall. I'll marry you." He was instantly off his knees and crushing her against his chest.

"I was sure I had lost you too. I didn't think you would give me a chance to talk to you. Mary said that for a long time you weren't taking phone calls." Brooke took as much of a breath as she could manage crushed against the falconer and put her arms around him as well.

"The only reason I talked to you was because I promised your mother that I would."

"What!" Marshall pushed Brooke an arm's-length away. "Alicia called you?"

"She makes you call her Alicia too?" Brooke giggled.

"Everyone calls her Alicia." Marshall sighed and shook his head.

"I thought if you were talking to your mother again, maybe you were serious about making some changes."

"It's more serious than you think. I've agreed to do some work with the family business."

"That's wonderful!"

"So you don't mind if I'm rich?" He raised his eyebrows at her and she shrugged.

"I would rather you weren't, especially since I won't even be able to tell people what my fiancé's family business actually is." She crossed her arms and pouted. Marshall laughed.

"Have you ever heard of Anthony Imports?"

"Are you kidding? That's my favorite store. *Your* family? No! There's got to be hundreds of them across the country!"

"Two hundred thirty to be exact, but the first one was here in Southern California. Alicia thinks I'll have an eye for new merchandise to import for the stores. She has seen my work in the homes of some prominent families and is very impressed. What sold me was when she mentioned that a little bit of travel and acquisition work might give me new ideas for my own pieces. So I agreed to help out some part-time."

"Well, I won't be able to travel with you right away. I'm going to law school to be an environmental attorney. Once I'm established though, I imagine it would be good for my practice to see some foreign conservation projects. It would be good for my photography career too." Brooke winked at him and he shook his head at her.

"You've got a few surprises up your sleeve as well."

"I guess I do." Brooke stopped for a moment and then asked quietly, "You'll still fly falcons, won't you?"

"Not only does hope wear feathers, but it springs eternal. I'll always fly falcons. I'll buy a baby peregrine from the Jensens this spring."

"Oh good, because I'm going to apprentice under Mary next season."

"Mary! I don't think so. You'll apprentice under me." He slipped the diamond on her finger and put an arm around her to lead her back to the apartment.

"I think Mary would say that I'm better off learning falconry from a woman."

"I guess if you want to apprentice under a dirt-hawker that's your business. You won't be able to fly a real bird until you're a general falconer anyway." He gave a squeeze around her ribs and a kiss on the cheek.

"I suppose a real bird is a peregrine?" She tilted her head at him, sure what the answer would be.

"What else?" Brooke recognized the haughty look on Marshall's face. It was the same royal gaze the fox had given her camera.

"Come on, Prince Charming. Let's go celebrate." They walked into her kitchen together and he spun her around to look him in the face.

"I'm no prince, Brooke, and I can't promise you that we'll always be happy. I can promise you that I love you and that I'll be your partner for life."

"Really, Marshall. That's all a girl wants."

"Then I'll do my best to make sure that's what you get." She had meant to tell him that she loved him and she had missed him, but the kiss that they shared in the kitchen said all of that and more.